YOU CANNOT HAVE ALL THE ANSWERS

and other stories...

Deepa Agarwal

olive turtle

NIYOGI BOOKS

Published by
NIYOGI BOOKS
Block D, Building No. 77
Okhla Industrial Area, Phase-I
New Delhi-110 020, INDIA
Tel: 91-11-26816301, 26818960
Email: niyogibooks@gmail.com
website: www.niyogibooksindia.com

Editor: Jyotika Mansata
Design: Nabanita Das
Cover Design: Geetali Baruah

ISBN: 978-93-86906-37-3
Publication: 2018

Printed at: Niyogi Offset Pvt. Ltd., New Delhi, India

For my daughters

Garima, **Sonali** and **Geetika**

Contents

Cradle Song

Some stories begin at the beginning and some at the end. And in some it's hard to say where the beginning is and where the end.

This is a story of seven sisters. Seven is a lucky number, no doubt. But I have never heard of seven sisters being considered lucky. Only, if by chance, those seven sisters happen to be blessed with a brother. Then they can, they are bound to consider themselves lucky beyond all shade of doubt.

My mother was one of those seven sisters. The fourth, the bang-in-the-middle sister, with three older than her and three younger. She was born when my grandmother was beginning to tire a little of only giving birth to daughters. Tire, but not despair. For, being a truly determined woman, I don't think she despaired even when the seventh daughter, my Meena *maasi*, was born.

It was like a battle with destiny for her, I think; a battle she was determined to win at all costs. So, grim, stony with purpose, fortified with the accumulated magic of all the prayers, the rituals and the fasts which had become a part of her life through all those contentious years, the predictions of numerous astrologers and the blessings of countless saints—even those which had not worked so far—she had tried again and a son was born, changing the fate of the seven sisters overnight. From being considered pitiful, almost doomed, they suddenly found themselves blessed.

Such is the power of a male child.

Now in this story of seven lucky sisters, another 'seven' intrudes. The seventh year of the fourth decade of the twentieth century—1947 to be exact. A year written in letters of gold and blood for our country. The most auspicious year of the century for the millions who were freed from foreign rule, and yet a most inauspicious one, for many would call it so—the uprooted ones, those who fled bag and bundle, fire and blood marking their trail, when one country was suddenly split into two.

My mother was eleven when her brother was born—whose birth she had awaited ever since she became aware of the importance of having brothers. She has a vivid memory of the event. The dancing, the singing, the distribution of largesse, the new clothes. She remembers her mother, bedecked, bejewelled, her tired face aglow, rocking the baby in a magnificent new cradle, the best that money could buy.

But just a few months later, the best that money could buy them was escape, flight, as they hurried, frantic to get away from the house that was no longer shelter but a death trap. To flee the city that was no longer home but hostile territory. Almost everything had to be abandoned, including the cradle, in which the youngest of the sisters had furtively rocked herself when the baby was elsewhere. She had not possessed a new cradle, not even too many new clothes—she mostly wore hand-me-downs. Good quality, expensive hand-me-downs, since my grandfather was a prosperous trader. But then, new clothes, new cradles have a smell, a magic of their own, which she had rarely experienced. She was the one who had howled, thrown a tantrum because the cradle had to be left behind. The baby brother of course, did not even know what he was being deprived of.

His mother's lap was soft enough. Her breast was readily offered to soothe him whenever he happened to howl. The motion of the train rocked him all the way. My mother remembers the press, the stench of bodies. The weeping, sometimes low, a bare whimper; sometimes loud, a lament or a whole-hearted protest against the fickleness of fortune. She remembers blood-stained clothes, staring eyes and an unreal, distant howling that the wind sucked up from God knows where to graze their spines, setting them all a-shiver. She remembers the old man who mumbled, thumbing his prayer beads ceaselessly. She thought of his importunities dripping, dripping into the ears of an obdurate deity, like drops of water wearing away a stone. She remembers humming a song to herself to block out all those horrible sounds. The cradle song that her mother crooned to put her baby brother to sleep. It was the only one she could recall at the moment.

Still, they considered themselves lucky when they arrived, the whole family—the parents, the seven lucky sisters and the luck-producing brother—intact, at the place of refuge. They arrived, their bodies still swaying, rocked by the motion of the train, the sobbing of the bereaved, the cries still ringing in their ears. The memory of the blood-stained garments remained fresh. The journey haunted their dreams, or rather their nightmares, for years.

My grandmother offered repeated prayers of gratitude to the Almighty who had let her baby survive that horrendous flight. My mother thought of those prayers as a kind of magic spell—charmed words that protected them against future disaster. She repeated them after her mother and felt safe, cared for.

The baby grew, though my grandmother found the milk in her breasts much reduced—because of the trauma perhaps, or the hardships of their new estate. But the baby grew, despite all this, thrived in fact, cared for by seven doting sisters, even the youngest who still missed the cradle and lived in a state of confusion, wondering when they would return to their own home. She talked to the baby, poured out all her puzzlement on him. He replied, babbling in a tongue only she could understand. His answers must have satisfied her, because after a while she reconciled herself to living in a verandah, where cooking, eating, sleeping—everything was done in the same place, instead of in a proper house with separate rooms.

The baby grew and the family, still rocking on their feet, tried to steady themselves, jam their shaky feet into the ground. Plant them firmly, permanently, like a seed that remains fixed in one particular place—so that they could kill the memory of that hateful movement. Like a seed that germinates, bonds itself with the earth, clutching at it with its stubborn insistent roots, thrusting its growing stem upwards, greedily sucking nurture and sunshine through its spreading leaves.

My grandfather, forgetting what he had possessed in the old country, what he had been, took up whatever work he could.

There was the family to feed and ultimately, those seven sisters to think about, provide for. In other words, marry off with decent dowries. Yes, a man with seven daughters can barely pause to take breath, leave alone waste time in bewailing his misfortune. To be fair, the sisters did their bit—those of them who were old enough to do so. They knitted, they sewed, and they embroidered—dutifully setting themselves to any kind of labour that could be turned into money. My mother thought of that work as a mound of coins piling up, growing till it carried them out of the verandah to a proper house, and their father from the pavement into a proper shop.

'The marvel is that it actually happened,' Mamma says. Her eyes are very shiny. I try to think of her, of my aunts, my grandfather and grandmother, leading difficult, deprived lives. Sometimes it's hard to believe, looking at the diamonds flashing on their fingers, in their ears. For they are all more or less prosperous, their lives run smoothly on wheels well-oiled with money. But when I watch my mother haggling with a vegetable vendor, reducing him to the rock-bottom price with a determination that seems disproportionate, I can feel the motion that swayed her feet, like a faint, disturbing breeze.

All the same, that time was far, far behind in the past especially for us children, the offspring of the seven lucky sisters. (Oddly enough, all of them had more sons than daughters. It was as if providence was trying to make up for past injustice.) To repeat, the time they had experienced belonged to the stuff of myth and legend for us. Folklore of sorts, a kind of warning of what could happen, but unreal, invariably unreal ... except when somebody wept, which did happen now and then when the old times were recalled. This made us feel uncomfortable, even a little annoyed with the person who gave way. Because what was the point of dredging up bad memories, deliberately making oneself unhappy?

So it seemed strange, unbelievable, when one day, Meena *maasi*, my youngest aunt, the one who had missed the cradle the most, asked, 'Would you like to go home?'

'Go home?' My mother paused in the act of conveying a samosa to her mouth. Meena *maasi* was visiting; they'd spent a lazy afternoon, just chatting, as they often did, being well-heeled ladies of leisure. 'B-but, I'm home, I mean—what do you mean?' She put the samosa down, confused, a little perturbed, it seemed to me.

I wondered why, because after all, Meena *maasi*, the youngest, prettiest and most prosperous, was a little—well—peculiar. Her doting husband indulged her, her sisters protected her, took care of her. She had been considered the luckiest of the sisters; she'd opened the way for the brother, so desperately longed for—as the old women said. True, this luck had deserted her at one point. But the habit persisted.

'Home ... I said ... Have you forgotten what home was like?' Meena *maasi's* eyes were teasingly mysterious as she bit into a samosa, licking the chutney from her fingers.

'Home ...' Mamma repeated. Her brow had clouded; she gazed apprehensively at Meena *maasi*. 'You can't mean ...'

'Yes, I do—the place where we were all born. Would you like to go there, visit it?'

'You can't be serious!'

'I am. Absolutely serious.' And anyone could make out from her face that she had never been more serious in her life. 'He says he can make arrangements. He has a contact ...'

'He' of course was the doting husband, the man who had the ability to make almost any kind of 'arrangement', who possessed almost any kind of useful 'contact'.

I could feel the goose pimples flare up, a prickly rash, as if I had suddenly brushed against a cactus plant. Mamma looked scared, her face had turned patchy—but how could she say 'No'?

It was the cradle that was drawing her there—I should have guessed. I should have remembered the strange look that came into her eyes when she talked about it, as if it were not an ordinary cradle but a talisman, something magical. Because what memories could that place hold for her, that place she referred to as 'home'? For home was here, wasn't it? I found it significant that the other aunts refused. Or rather, found some ready excuse not to go. They began to make them even before they were asked, which made them look quite sheepish when Meena *maasi* said, 'I wasn't planning to take you all. Even *he* won't be able to make arrangements for so many people.'

I managed to tag along. I don't know why I went. I'm not sure if one really wants to know what one's mother's life was like before she became your mother. It interferes too much with the image that's familiar, that means mother. But perhaps a time comes in life when the need to know overcomes that insecurity. When one is afraid that the chance will be lost forever if one postpones too much.

Because it did interfere with the image. My mother's hysterical, excited reunion with what remained of the old world that she had known—neighbours, shopkeepers, even an old childhood friend—was in sharp contrast to her normal demeanour, of the controlled, level-headed person I had always known her to be.

Tears were shed. Long-buried memories disinterred. Meena *maasi* was quiet though. After having thought about, planned, arranged and anticipated everything—was there a sense of anti-climax? Or, not being able to conjure up common memories, renew bonds, was she feeling a little left out?

It didn't help when I tactlessly whispered, 'You couldn't be remembering anything, could you?'

Her eyes flashed with affront. 'Of course I do, it's all there ... deep inside ...'

It was at that very moment that the old lady entered. An amazingly fat old lady, her silks rustling and swishing, panting and sweating from excitement and exertion.

'Kanta! Kanta, is it really you? Ah, what a miracle! I heard that you were here. I couldn't believe it! No one, no one has come back—even for a visit.'

'Saida *bua*! It's Saida *bua*!' Mamma exclaimed. 'It's hard,' she sighed. 'Almost impossible ...' The rest of her words were squashed out by Saida *bua's* embrace.

'Who's this? Not Meena, not little Meena ... And—your daughter? Amazing, wonderful!' More embraces, laughter and tears. Then she paused, pinned Mamma with a look full of happy, satisfied meaning. 'Come, come on, you have to come to my house. At once!' she commanded, taking my mother's hand, almost dragging her away. Helpless, laughing, Mamma allowed herself to be led away. We followed, bemused.

'I have something to show you,' she muttered. 'You'll get such a surprise. Your mother should have come. Why didn't you bring her?'

Mamma mumbled the same excuse she had been giving to everyone. Old age, the rigours of travel, the danger of too much excitement. Meena *maasi* frowned, touched her forehead delicately, as if all this talk was giving her a headache. We sat down gingerly on the plush sofa, swallowed more syrupy sherbet, nibbled at some more sweets.

'You won't believe it ...' Saida *bua* sighed. 'You know ... after you all went away ...' she broke off abruptly, as if reconsidering the suitability of what she was about to say. Then ended by muttering, 'Ah, what a dreadful time it was ... terrible, unbelievable. The looting, the destruction ... But I managed ...' She threw a quick glance at Mamma's face, which was turning grim, and hurriedly switched tracks to say, 'Your daughter looks just like your mother. What a lovely woman—so brave, so generous ... *Oye*, Rehman, bring it fast!' she yelled suddenly.

Meena *maasi* blinked, sat up nervously, when we heard the sound of something being dragged down the stairs. Something heavy, something wooden?

'Let it be, let it be,' Mamma half rose, with smiling politeness. 'Don't trouble yourself ...' But did her brow knit with sudden anxiety?

'No, no, you must see it—did you dust it properly? I saved it from the looters, kept it all these years ... in the hope that someone from your family might come—and now you have.' She beamed as if she had achieved some prize objective. 'It's a precious thing, so auspicious, I wouldn't give it away—though many people begged me for it. Something told me, I knew you would come one day ...'

But Mamma had gone wooden, she wasn't listening anymore and actually neither were we—Meena *maasi* and I—at least not properly.

'Ah, If only you could take it back for your brother—why didn't he come? Kake ... That's what you used to call him, how little he was ... He could use it for his son—how many—Oh, don't, please don't ...'

It was Meena *maasi* who had darted forward. My mother still stood there, as if carved out of wood. Then, as I also started up, I heard her wailing ... a sound so anguished that it tied my guts into innumerable painful knots.

Yes, it was the cradle. A solid heavy, old-fashioned cradle. Streaks of ancient dust had embedded themselves in the intricately carved wood. But, in a strange inexplicable way, it still looked remarkably new and unused.

Saida *bua* was clinging to Mamma and wailing too. Then I heard Meena *maasi's* voice buzzing in my ears. My eyes were blurring, but I could see that hers were hard and glazed as she said, stroking it over and over again, 'I used to rock in it when he wasn't lying inside. I remember ... I remember ... I remember ...'

I grabbed her hand, squeezed it as hard as I could. I had to make her stop. She accused me later of having jabbed her with my nails. I might have. The moment was so charged, so desperate ...

She was humming a tune on the flight back. A tune I knew very well. It was a lullaby my mother had sung to us as babies. It made me feel a little sick now.

'Thank God—' Mamma began when Meena *maasi* interrupted her.

'Poor old woman … Do you really believe that the cradle was lucky? I cannot. But you're right. It was a good thing that we were able to keep it from her … that Kake wasn't alive any more … that he died before he could get married … before he could have kids to place in that cradle …'

'What is lucky, unlucky?' Mamma said, sniffing back her tears. 'Who really knows?' Her voice seemed to choke up.

But Meena *maasi* interrupted. 'Are you going to tell *Biji* that we—that I've brought the cradle back? Maybe we'd better not … I don't know. Anyway, I'm going to keep it …'

I was the one who gasped aloud. But Mamma made no reply. She just stared at Meena *maasi* as if she were seeing her for the first time … Meena *maasi* smiled back faintly … triumphantly, perhaps.

I wanted to ask her why she had agreed to, insisted rather, on bringing it back if she really didn't think it was lucky. In spite of Mamma's hesitation, her misgivings. In spite of the trouble, the inconvenience of transporting it. Of course, she had her husband's 'contact', who had smoothed the way.

It hadn't occurred to me that she wanted it for herself.

Why? To revive a cherished memory … or compensate herself for some lingering sense of grievance? Or just to take possession of the new-old cradle which had never been hers … but which she had wanted so passionately.

And suddenly it struck me that they were right, after all, the old women. For all her strangeness, she had been the lucky one after all. And she had known it ... somehow she had known it, deep inside—the seventh sister. She had known it would be hers ... finally ...

The Back Verandah

'Do you think Kusum is a nymphomaniac?' Saroj didi—Niloo's older sister, a knowledgeable twenty-three—asked, her voice crisp and sure with the authority of her college teacher's job.

The words had the bludgeoning resonance of a gong. So strong that it obliterated Papa's response. Chewing mechanically on her piece of toast—her father's face stretched into a seeming smile, his look of weary patience clearly imprinted, but his voice oddly soundless—twelve-year-old Niloo considered the word. Nymphomaniac. The exact meaning remained unclear. But not the threatening, almost criminal connotation. Kusum's face materialised in her mind. The over-bright, grey-brown eyes, the small, regular teeth, even the lank hair that swung about her chin had acquired a faint, somewhat interesting menace.

Confusion followed. The early morning light, pouring in through the skylight, turned dazzling and upset the cool, walled-in ambience of the shabby old dining room. Wasn't Kusum a pleasant, no a fascinating companion? Didn't her mother encourage her to visit their house? And why did she get the feeling that Saroj didi's intent was to provoke, perhaps challenge; that the question was not really a question, but a statement.

Suddenly her father's voice became audible, like an echo returning. She had heard him, of course, but her mind had put it away somewhere, temporarily. 'Her father was the same,' he said. The response seemed spontaneous, almost a reflex action. Uneasily she realised that in a way he was ratifying Saroj didi's statement. But also deflecting her attack, perhaps. Because, everything considered—it was an attack, wasn't it?

Kusum's father—cadaverous, gap-toothed, a fringe of grey-white hair edging his smooth, bald head. Shabby in unpressed pants, shirts that were missing buttons. The flavour of the guava jelly she'd smeared so liberally on her toast was unpleasantly strong suddenly. Could something like that be inherited?

'What is a nymphomaniac?' she asked loudly, to get rid of the taste on her tongue. But repeating the words only seemed to reinforce it.

She heard Papa's suppressed gasp, caught the look of helpless disapproval he threw at Saroj didi. Saw the almost imperceptible shake of his head. He'd forgotten that she was there. Poor Papa. He tried hard, so hard to keep Saroj didi in good humour. It never worked, though, and didn't now. She ignored him, keeping her head haughtily averted.

Instead she turned to Niloo. 'Someone who likes men too much—in a bad way,' she said slowly, as though weighing her words. With an air of grim martyrdom, as if, however much she hated it, certain things had to be explained to Niloo. She did glance at Papa now from beneath her lashes—which were long and so extravagantly curling that they were visible, even behind her glasses. They looked out of place on that thin, small-featured face, as if they had landed there by mistake. 'A bad girl,' she added.

'Now, now,' Papa said quickly, clearing his throat. He looked distinctly perturbed. There was a crease between his heavy brows, his long jaw sagged. A sigh burst from him like a whiff of some deep, underlying sadness. 'That's not a 100 per cent correct, you know. Kusum isn't really a—.' He cleared his throat delicately, as if making an attempt to smudge out the word. 'She's—well, a little too friendly—maybe.' His voice was barely audible.

Niloo's head swung towards Saroj didi on its own. Her face had a faint sneer, a tight, closed-up expression, as if she couldn't or wouldn't give any credence to Papa's words. And in a way, she was right, because he had backed up her statement originally—hadn't he? Niloo prepared to edge out of her chair. She didn't like this conversation. There were too many undercurrents, unpleasant ones, she could guess from Papa's face.

'Likes men in a bad way ...' What was a good way? Saroj didi and Pratap bhaiya, perhaps. Playing badminton together, chatting on the front verandah. Sort of brotherly and sisterly—after all, his father was an old family friend.

Kusum was an outcaste of sorts, she knew. She'd done something terrible—eloped with a boy. Strange, it seemed now to Niloo, that her father should have gone after her and hauled her back, even as they were preparing to get married. At least, that's what Kusum said.

She'd been properly ostracised after her return by everyone except Niloo's mother. Ma wasn't there at the breakfast table right now. She was busy with something in the garden. But Niloo wouldn't have put it past Saroj didi to have said it to her face. She never cared what she said to Ma or Papa. Maybe it was her way of showing that she was grown up, no longer dependent on them. Not that she'd have gotten any kind of response from their mother. She'd have acted as if Saroj hadn't spoken at all. And Papa wouldn't have replied either in that case.

As she got up from the table, Niloo could imagine the possible scene. Saroj didi fermenting silently, her fine face reddening, her eyelids flapping like an agitated moth's wings behind her glasses.

She had already slipped out of the room when she heard the call, 'You haven't finished your toast!' Niloo quickened her step, hurried on to the verandah where the sunlight was spreading itself out, threatening the small geometrical patch of shade that remained.

It pressed against her eyes, making her feel as lethargic as the bees buzzing hazily around the *kamini* bush outside. Just a few, though there'd be swarms in the evening. The weariness seemed to overcome her, she longed for the cool, scented evening. If only the day could be rubbed out—like a mistake from a copy-book—and evening be written in instead. Then she started, as she heard someone breathe heavily behind her. 'Why did you leave the breakfast table without finishing your toast?'

Niloo felt the weight dragging her down but kept her face innocent and bland. 'I'd finished eating.' She watched Saroj didi's sari *pallu* swinging behind her, like a pendulum set in motion by her own hurried steps. A green, *kota* sari, well starched, too nice for just spending the day at home.

'Hunh,' she wasn't sure if it was an expression of agreement or disapproval. Sometimes she felt Saroj didi was everything a strict mother would have been. As if she felt it was her duty to make up for Ma's tolerance, her ability to absorb the most flagrant misdemeanour calmly. And then it came, 'By the way, you shouldn't talk to her so much.' Her voice was low, controlled as ever. But—did Niloo sense that same disturbing resonance? 'All that giggling and whispering in corners. She isn't your age to be friends with ... She's not a nice girl, Niloo.'

Niloo turned. Saroj didi's face was expressionless, her eyes did not censure. It was not as if she was blaming Niloo. Just telling her what the right thing was. But Niloo felt embarrassed, she didn't know why. As if by association something of Kusum had rubbed off onto her. There was also a faint, uneasy flare of rebellion. Ma never said anything, why did she have to interfere?

I will, I will, she repeated to herself as she ran out, letting the summer sun smite her face. It had a harsh, clean force unlike Saroj didi's words which seemed to quiver and dart as if not quite sure what they wanted to hit, destroy. And then it came to her—why didn't she call Kusum, 'Kusum didi'? She was much older than her—eighteen to be exact. Was it because of her diminished social status? Did that particular episode—or whatever tendencies she possessed, tendencies that could justify Saroj didi's epithet—bring her down to Niloo's level?

Not that the ostracism seemed to bother her too much. Niloo had heard the story of her elopement, narrated like an account of a trip to the movies. Told without shame, as Niloo's mother sat in the verandah entertaining an acquaintance.

Ma had been sitting on a round-backed cane chair. Mrs Prasad faced her on its matching counterpart. Cups of tea, chocolate biscuits—Niloo had been munching on one—stood on a table between them. Kusum sat on a *moorah*, embroidering a table cloth. She had a fine hand for such work and Ma encouraged her, getting cloth and thread for her to work with. Actually, she had been doing this kind of work for Ma before she took off. She'd been a BA student then. After that her studies had come to an end. Her father had a good excuse not to send her back to college. No one had bothered to offer her any chocolate biscuits, not even Niloo. She wanted to, and suffered as she munched one. It felt dry, stuck to her palate, but her hand felt too heavy and weak to pick up the plate and pass it to Kusum. Or maybe it was her mind.

Actually, Kusum hadn't volunteered the information. It was Mrs Prasad who asked her, in a hoarse, accusing sort of a voice, 'So where all have you been roaming, hunh? How could you think of doing such a thing? Aren't you ashamed of yourself?'

Niloo had noticed the way her mouth had pursed when she arrived, knitting bag in hand, and saw Kusum sitting there, head bent over her sewing. 'So, you've put her to work?' she'd remarked, with a look full of malice. Ma had nodded in a bored, indifferent sort of a way. As if Kusum's presence there was as unremarkable as the maid, Kalyani's, who was picking wheat a little distance away. The truth was, entertaining Kusum was an unforgivable social blunder in their small town—a place where someone like her would not be forgiven easily.

Kusum had given a literal reply. Deliberately, Niloo suspected. She'd laughed, causing Mrs Prasad to start. 'I wanted to—we-we wanted to ...' her head snapped up, her pale eyes glinting at Mrs Prasad, looking her full in the face. She giggled shamelessly. 'I crept out at 12:30. I'd flung two changes into a bag and hidden it—I didn't want anyone getting suspicious.' She had smiled in a conspiratorial way as if making them all party to her adventure. Mrs Prasad had frowned, but perhaps her curiosity had prevented her from protesting. 'It was pitch dark,' Kusum went on. 'Rakesh, like a fool, hadn't even brought a torch. We tripped and rolled down the hill as we were running off.'

She'd giggled uncontrollably as she said this. Her shoulders loosened, the table cloth slipped off her lap. Mrs Prasad had made a choking sound. Her sari *pallu* had slipped off her shoulder too. It often did—exposing a frightening expanse of cleavage. Niloo never missed an opportunity to get a good eyeful. There was something fascinating about that deep crevice. As if it held some enticing mystery within it.

But right then even she had felt outraged at Kusum's audacity at reducing something so shameful into a joke. But beneath that outrage there was a sickening excitement. She could see them rolling down the hill, their bodies touching, piling up in a heap on top of each other. She'd glanced up at her mother quickly, wanting her to censure, admonish Kusum. But her mother sat there, impassive. Her mouth had twitched faintly. Was she suppressing a smile or an impulse to scold Kusum? Niloo had felt let down, diminished in front of that cat Mrs Prasad, who would no doubt spread the story all over town.

Even Kalyani had snorted. Kusum's smile had lost its brassy glaze then, become a little fixed as if she didn't know what to do with it. She, too, had glanced at Ma in an appealing sort of way, as if asking for some kind of support. But Ma had merely looked abstracted, lost in distant thought.

Mrs Prasad, on the other hand, had clicked her knitting needles venomously and said, '*Besharam*! You should be ashamed to show your face. Anyone else would have drowned themselves instead of going about all plastered with powder, dressed to kill. How does your mother allow it?'

She had glared at Niloo's mother who'd jerked back to life, murmuring something vague like, 'She's just a young girl ...', hurriedly picked up her tea cup and gulped down the cold dregs that remained.

Kusum's face had been inflamed. She'd opened her mouth to speak, then she'd glanced at Niloo's mother and stopped as if she'd received some hidden message. After a long, breathless moment she'd got up instead and whispered to Niloo, 'Come. Let's play cards.'

Niloo had gone reluctantly. She'd found Mrs Prasad's outburst as annoying as Ma's failure to put Kusum in her place. She was not quite sure whether it was something she could accept, the fact that Ma had appointed herself Kusum's champion. She couldn't speak out against it openly—like Saroj didi, who seldom lost a chance. Especially when everyone else had barred their doors to her. Did it mean that Ma condoned Kusum's behaviour? Surely she didn't. Was it just plain bravery—standing up for someone, whom everybody condemned? And that was one thing she was very unsure about—Ma's bravery. Could someone as silent and passive as her be considered brave? Or was it something in the same line as sending the sweeper's children to school, passing on old clothes and leftover food? And Kusum—did she really deserve or need that kind of support?

'*Churail, haramzadi*,' Kusum said as she shuffled the cards clumsily.

'Kusum!' Niloo cried out severely, 'If you abuse in front of me, I'll tell Ma.' Even though she felt a liberating excitement gush up inside her. There was something so wonderfully devil-may-care about words like these. 'And ... You're dropping all the cards.' She was still chafing at the fact that she'd been compelled to range herself on Kusum's side in front of Mrs Prasad. But she didn't have the heart to reject that appeal—which it certainly was. Because—and this was something that made her really uncomfortable at times—she couldn't help liking Kusum.

'I'll tell Ma,' Kusum had mimicked, her face blackening. 'No, no, don't get annoyed. Can't I joke once in a while?'

Niloo had jerked her head away, torn between fury and fascination. She'd pounced on her cards and frowned at them, avoiding Kusum's glittering, mesmerising eyes. Her pale, taut, thin-lipped face. But a few minutes later she'd been rolling in her chair as Kusum reproduced Mrs Prasad's tone of voice with cruel perfection. She'd even run into the dining room silently and brought the whole tin of chocolate biscuits, which they'd devoured with gusto.

So what if she isn't my age, she thought now, running towards the back verandah. It would be cool and shady there, flanked as it was by two large trees, bordered with numerous overgrown bushes. A place where Saroj didi never went. She'd encountered a snake there once, she said. Niloo would be safe. Safe to sit and think.

But, as she approached, she heard voices. Two of them. Kusum's and another—a man's voice.

Niloo halted, overcome by curiosity as well as a vague dread. The man's voice was low, just a murmur. Kusum's laugh rang out shrill and metallic, though. It sounded different, somehow. It made her uneasy. Churned something up inside her, set little prickles of sensation zipping down her skin. Zipping, prickling—all gathering together to accumulate in that one particular spot between her legs ...

Breathless, she wondered, biting down on her lower lip, letting those feelings ripple up and down her in pleasurable waves ... what was Kusum doing there so early today? She normally arrived in the afternoon and stayed on till the evening. And the man, who was he?

She edged forward, trying to keep her breath even. Then stopped. Did she want to see who it was? Suppose, suppose they were doing something, something she ought not to see? She felt a tight, stuffy fullness in her chest. Then a sudden, tearing hatred for Kusum. Nymphomaniac. The word surfaced, knocking against her head. Nymphomaniac, she hissed, feeling as venomous as the snake that had frightened Saroj didi. Tearfully desperate, she tiptoed ahead.

Kusum's laugh rang out again. The man's followed—in an awful complementary sort of a way. Was there some kind of a sound—a sort of shuffling, scuffling? But already Niloo could feel her skin harden around her, setting like an icy case. She had recognised the laugh. It was Pratap, Pratap bhaiya, she should say. She shouldn't have gone further, she knew, but she couldn't stop herself. She wanted to be sure—absolutely sure. And just as she stepped forward, the lizard appeared. It darted out from nowhere—across her path, almost touching her foot.

After that she was conscious only of the shrieks filling her ears and Kusum and Pratap bhaiya's frightened faces. Kusum's eyes unreal, like a stuffed tiger's, bulging from their kaajaled outline. The minute beads of sweat on her upper lip so close she could have counted them. And she could not help noticing that her chunni was missing, the buttons of her kurta open, exposing that dark, deep cleft, making her want to reach out and put her hand inside. As if that would solve the mystery, eventually. And Pratap bhaiya ... He looked strange too, his nostrils dilating, his chest moving up and down as his breath came out in little panting gulps ... as though something inside him was expanding, expanding ... and would explode any minute.

Then she began to laugh, helplessly, uncontrollably. 'It was nothing, nothing,' she said. 'Just a *girgatang*. I got scared ... uh ... Where did you all come from?' She eased her arm out of Pratap bhaiya's hard, warm grip. It rested too close against the side of her chest, too close to her tiny bosom.

He turned his head and mumbled something. Kusum remained silent, tight-lipped. She really puts too much powder, Niloo thought. It stood out whitely on her wheatish skin. She didn't look pretty any more.

'If you're looking for Saroj didi, she's inside,' she told Pratap bhaiya, who nodded vigorously and turned towards the house.

'You've come very early,' she flung at Kusum, who shrugged jerkily but still didn't reply.

Half an hour later, though, Niloo found her perched quite placidly on her *moorah* on the verandah. God knows what happened to Pratap bhaiya. Neither he nor Saroj didi were anywhere around. 'What's this now?' Niloo asked, looking at the new piece Kusum was working on.

'A bedcover,' she said, without looking up.

'A bedcover ... for whom?' She knew very well for whom, she asked just to keep the conversation going.

'For your sister's trousseau,' Kusum said. She looked up now and laughed. An ugly laugh, like a piece of cloth ripping.

'Her trousseau?' Niloo exclaimed. 'But she's not getting married.' This statement too, was superfluous, she knew. Her sister's trousseau had no connection with a marriage date being fixed. It was, had been in the process of preparation for quite some time, in spite of Saroj didi's protests, her scorn for such things.

'She's hoping to, I expect,' Kusum laughed again. She bit off the thread with a vicious jerk.

Niloo felt the hatred rear up again. She squeezed it down, carefully. 'And what about you,' she said insinuatingly. 'Aren't you hoping to get married too? Why aren't you preparing your own trousseau?'

Kusum's face darkened. 'I would have been married by now,' she said. 'If it hadn't been for my stupid father!' Niloo was shocked at the throb in her voice. 'I would have been far away ...' She sniffed, the pale eyes filled up, spilled over.

Niloo didn't know what to say. Was she expected to console her, because she hadn't been able to do something everyone said was wrong, horribly wrong? Confusion swept over her again. Maybe it was that confusion that made her ask, in a soft, confidential tone, 'What were you doing back there ...?'

Kusum stared at her, her eyes like marbles. Her lips were beginning to draw back from her teeth when Niloo, panicking, whispered, 'Are you really a nymphomaniac?'

The moment she said it she knew she'd done something unbelievably, irretrievably foolish. Disastrous, in fact. Something perhaps a child half her age might have better sense not to do. But it was their entire fault, she thought later. Saroj didi's and Papa's and Ma's and Pratap bhaiya's and of course, Kusum's. Most of all Kusum's. For being one.

She would never forget how Kusum repeated it, though. 'N-nymphomaniac ...?' her thin, dark lipsticked mouth expanding and hissing as perhaps a snake's might. 'Who—who said it? Tell me—who said it?' Her pale eyes held Niloo's frightened ones so close that she felt the moment of understanding shoot through her, like a bolt of electricity consuming both of them. A sob burst out, large and so plangent that Ma heard it and came out— just in time to receive the rest of Kusum's fury.

Yes, Niloo would never forget it—the bedcover coming flying at Ma, like a sail torn from its moorings. 'Let her make it herself, her wretched trousseau—if anyone will ever agree to marry her!' And as Ma stared at her astounded: 'Whatever I may be, I'm better than her! My parents were married at least ...'

Ma swayed, she might have fallen, Niloo rushed forward to catch her, but she righted herself. 'Kusum, Kusum, child, what's the matter?' she said weakly. Her arms reached out after Kusum, who was already stomping off. They dropped helplessly then. She sagged into a chair, her eyes closed, her body limp.

'Ma! Ma!' Niloo cried, overcome by an appalling guilt and an even more terrifying fear. 'Can I get you a glass of water?'

She ran off without waiting for a reply, but not before she'd come face to face with Saroj didi and Pratap bhaiya. Saroj didi's eyes were enormous behind her glasses, her mouth wasn't working. Pratap bhaiya managed to look baffled and guilty at the same time.

It was later ... much later. Kusum had left, fled—no, not fled—she'd stomped off, leaving a trail of invective behind her. The same words she'd used for Mrs Prasad. They made Niloo feel sick, loathsome now. Niloo stood at the door of her mother's room. She wanted to go in there, say something, but she didn't know what ... how ... And when she heard Saroj didi's voice, she halted, of course. 'Now he knows—thanks to her. How could you let her into the house—how did she know? Does everybody in this town know—that I ...?' Her voice had crumpled up after that. Lost that unassailable confidence, which was so much a part of her that Niloo couldn't imagine her without it. 'I-I thought you'd come here because—How could you do it?' Her voice jerking out, an acid, hurtful, spray, showering Ma with hateful words. She'd heard the sound of stifled weeping and Ma's anguished reply.

'Ssshssh, *beti*. Don't say that! Don't ever say that!'

Niloo stood outside, shaking. She could see Ma's tears falling too, silently, ceaselessly, even though there was a door between them. Sometimes, however, one can see through walls. She had felt a pain in her belly so sharp and acute, that she doubled up and almost screamed.

Of course, Kusum never came again. In fact she never went anywhere, just like Mrs Prasad and many others wanted. Niloo wondered if it was a kind of justice when she caught a glimpse of her outside her house as she passed that way once—her belly grotesquely swollen, her clothes shabby and careless, her face plain and lifeless, bereft of makeup. But it also filled her with a terrible fear. Because suddenly, Kusum's face vanished and another superimposed itself. And she found herself running, running, till she realised it was futile. After all, she had to go home.

Saroj didi had probably been seized with a similar impulse. She had run too, and taken up a job in a college in a big city. Ma had been silent, impassive as ever. Papa was the one who'd looked broken. 'I always considered you my own child,' he'd whispered, when Saroj didi was leaving. But she'd said nothing. The only time she showed emotion was when she hugged Niloo.

Niloo might not have recognised her but for those extra-bright eyes. A hefty, overdressed matron, with two children in tow. She had quickly suppressed the thought that had sprung up on its own ... which one?

She'd reached out to embrace Niloo, who had been trying to turn away, with enthusiasm. She'd been stiff in that embrace with the remnants of that old ambivalence haunting her. And of course, the scar of that old memory, which had changed so much for her. Too much.

But Kusum wouldn't let go. She rambled on—as if all that had never happened. As if they were really old friends meeting after a long time. Maybe she wanted to remember it like that. But then the moment had come. She had asked softly, 'How's your sister?'

After Niloo had replied, told her about Saroj didi's successful, meaningful life, she'd said with a sigh, 'I wanted to come and meet your mother so many times ... but ...' she'd looked Niloo in the face with an anxious, no, a desperate insistence, 'I never told anyone. Tell your mother—I never told anyone. It's such an odd thing ...' her face became still and thoughtful. 'Rakesh—the fellow whom I ran away with—', here she giggled in the old careless way. 'His sister told me. We were staying with her when—you know, when.' Her smile had been wry, but good humoured. 'She'd known your mother a long time back. When it happened, before she met your father and came to live in this town.'

Niloo felt the old shame rear up, wrap around her like a scaly skin. She had not told Kusum that they didn't have much part in Saroj didi's life. None of them, certainly not Ma, or bewildered, well-meaning Papa. Niloo, perhaps. But not enough.

She tried to conjure up the old hatred, but couldn't. Odd, she thought, time can eat up hatred, but shame is indigestible.

But not for Kusum, perhaps, because after she moved away, she heard the old coquettish laugh ring out. She half turned her head, unable to resist the curious impulse and saw the broad back, the grey head of a middle-aged man. And she could see those pale eyes glinting. She felt the old confusion again as Saroj didi's epithet surfaced. Was she right in a way? Small comfort, she thought, considering the price she'd paid, they'd all paid—for her naïveté, her need to show off and Saroj didi's need to get even with Ma.

You Cannot Have All the Answers

'You cannot have all the answers,' said the wise woman. 'All I can say is, you're going in the wrong direction, foolish one.' She was a very wise old woman who had lived long and could even look into the future.

'You may be right, old mother,' replied the foolish one. 'But ... perhaps I'm not looking for answers—maybe, I want the question to remain a question. To embark on a quest that never attains its goal. For what can be better than striving endlessly? Striving for something which may not be there?'

'You are wasting your life then, foolish one,' said the wise woman. 'Give up. There are goals which can be fulfilled. Quests that can be ended. Questions answered.'

'A question that is answered means the end. A goal fulfilled is death. I want to live, wise mother,' the foolish one answered.

'You are the bravest of the brave. Go, I grant you the boon of unrequited love.' The wise woman plucked a wilted flower from her hair and gave it to the foolish one, who went forth joyfully.

She would become the moth who singed her wings against the flame. She would become the nightingale sighing for the moon.

But the wise woman sighed too. Another promising soul lost.

Who was the wise woman? And who was the foolish one? We anticipate, perhaps. For, unlike what the old woman said, time answers all questions—or practically all.

Mandira ran down the steps on to the road, twirling the wilted flower in her hand. She wanted to laugh. How amazingly appropriate the gift was! Unrequited love! She was ready to embrace the role of the rejected lover. She would write beautiful poetry, sing sad songs and sigh like a veritable furnace. She saw herself standing at her window, her hair streaming down her back, gazing at the moon. How wonderfully romantic it would be! As romantic as marriage was prosaic. She thought of her parents and pulled a face. How unbearably dull their life together was. Dal, subzi, roti and balancing accounts. She definitely didn't want to end up like that!

A beggar woman approached her, her face split by a theatrical grimace of woe, whining for a coin. Mandira exclaimed with annoyance. She'd forgotten her purse at home. Laughingly, irreverently, she dumped the flower that was the wise woman's *prasad* into the beggar's tin can. The beggar woman growled, then sucked in her breath in astonishment. The moment the flower touched the can, it clinked. It had turned into a coin, a shining new gold coin. Unable to believe her eyes, she ran after Mandira, who had walked off, striding swiftly as was her wont. She managed to catch up.

A little annoyed, Mandira waved her hands in the air to show that she had nothing else. The beggar woman folded her hands, actually in thanks, but Mandira mistook it to be a plea for more. Glancing around, exasperated, she noticed a young man coming along. He looked like a nice, pleasant fellow. 'Excuse me,' she said in her forthright way. She was like that, always very direct and straightforward. 'Do you have a coin to give this beggar woman?'

The young man was a little taken aback. He had never had a young woman accosting him in the street like that, asking for alms for someone else. But he really was a nice young man and her eager, mobile face with its tendrils of hair floating about it moved him so much that he had to give the beggar woman something. He took out a ten-rupee note and let it flutter into the tin. The beggar woman was overwhelmed. She fell at Mandira's feet, much to her added annoyance.

'Really, this is too much,' she said, shaking her head. 'She should be falling at your feet. Thanks awfully, by the way. I forgot my purse at home. Just like me. Terribly absent-minded, I am.'

The young man beamed. It seemed a delightful quality to him. But Mandira was already turning away. Stop! He wanted to cry out. I have so many things to ask you. But the moment was already slipping away. Their little transaction had come to an end. Then, as luck would have it, he saw something flutter down from her hand. Was it a hankie? What a god-sent opportunity! This was classic, absolutely classic. He dived forward. But as he was about to pick it up he realised it was a tissue.

He could have gnashed his teeth. How foolish of him. No one used handkerchiefs any longer. What was the protocol with regard to tissues? Would she take offence if he picked it up and gave it to her? Would it be like an accusation of littering? But she must have definitely dropped it by mistake. She didn't look like a litterbug. He was positive she was environmentally aware. This young man, by the way, whose name was Samir, was a committed environmentalist and hated litterbugs. Anyway, since this was the only chance he had of continuing his contact with her, he decided to take the risk.

But no sooner had he scooped that crumpled little tissue up, his eyes almost popped out. Even as he watched, it transformed itself into a beautiful silk scarf. Truly, it was a day for miracles, though little did Mandira, the innocent cause, know!

Samir blinked, shook his head, pinched himself to make sure that he was awake. Then he made a sensible decision. He decided that some kind fairy had decided to take care of his interests and so he ought to proceed in the matter, which he did by running after Mandira and telling her that she'd dropped the silk scarf.

'Oh,' she said frowning. 'Did I drop this? Hmmm—I didn't realise I was wearing this. I must be more absent-minded than I realise. Thanks again. It really must be my lucky day, meeting you.'

Samir's smile grew even wider. 'Please, please,' he said quickly before she walked off again. 'Can you have a cup of coffee with me?'

Mandira sighed. She really was not in the mood to have cups of coffee with strange young men. But ... actually ... she should be if she was to avail of her boon of unrequited love. It would give her the opportunity to fall in love with someone who would no doubt spurn her later on. But this was not one of the things she generally did—having cups of coffee with strange young men. In fact she was extraordinarily particular about it. But today was a different sort of a day. She had met the wise woman, she had met the beggar woman and now this young man. Maybe something was meant to come out of this meeting.

Well, as it so happened, something did.

More meetings, to begin with, and many more cups of coffee and lunches and then dinners. But it always puzzled Mandira that Samir would invariably ask her to give him her used up bits of tissue. She thought it some strange quirk in his make-up, albeit a harmless one. She also wondered how she happened to drop a scarf that day. She never used them. In fact she didn't possess a single one. Perhaps it was one of those ploys young men used to get acquainted with a young woman. She forgave him for that of course. It is always flattering to know that a man is interested enough in you to resort to such tricks. But she couldn't help wondering, did he always roam around with a pretty silk scarf in his pocket in the hope of coming across a girl who caught his fancy? It seemed rather calculating, and also made him appear a kind of beast always on the prowl. But he had such a charming smile and such long-lashed brown eyes that it was easy to forgive him a lot.

Samir on the other hand could never decide if he had witnessed a genuine magical happening or whether he had been hallucinating that day. He became even more confused when she asked him one day with a twinkle in her eye, where he had got the scarf he picked up that day.

'From the ground,' he said. 'You-you dropped it.'

'Did I?' she asked and laughed.

A lot of time had passed since that first fateful meeting. Yes, a lot of water had passed under the bridge of their relationship. Now it had reached the stage where she had taken him home to meet her parents and he had taken her home to meet his. Things had gone amicably. No objections had been raised on either side. The two had even begun to look at rings.

But when Mandira laughed in that particular manner, Samir couldn't help feeling stung. In the first place he had never gotten over his confusion about the tissue changing into the silk scarf. As they had become more intimate he had waited for Mandira to open up and tell him more about it. He had looked out for more magical happenings to occur and when they hadn't, his confusion had grown. Part of Mandira's charm, part of the adventure of knowing her was the prospect that something extraordinary could happen. When it didn't, Samir couldn't help feeling slightly cheated. And yet he continued with the relationship in the hope that someday it might.

So he retaliated by saying, 'Don't you know where the scarf came from?'

'How can I?' Mandira shot back. 'I never possessed a scarf like that.'

'You-you didn't—'

'You know that, don't you?'

'I-I don't know.'

'Oh stop it! Come clean!'

'What are you trying to say?'

'That you pretended the scarf was mine!' Mandira was nothing if not blunt. 'I must say you're quite a character, going around with scarves in your pocket to snare girls.'

'Snare girls with scarves in my pocket—' Samir spluttered. 'How dare you! You dropped the scarf.'

'I don't need to resort to such cheap tricks.'

'Yes, you do.' In his heart of hearts he knew it was unfair, that she had not dropped the scarf, that she really did not need to resort to such tricks—at least as far as he was concerned. He had felt attracted to her before the scarf incident. But her accusation made him see red.

Well, as it often happens with such arguments, they parted in a rage. Because Samir could hardly tell her that a tissue she had dropped had magically turned into a silk scarf. If she wasn't aware of it, wouldn't she have laughed at him if he'd said that?

Broken-hearted, Mandira decided to visit the wise woman again. She wanted to confirm that this was what she had meant when she had conferred the boon of unrequited love on her. But when she went to her house, she found the door locked. Sadly she came back to the street when the same beggar woman, who had haunted the place since then, hoping to find her again, caught sight of her. She rushed forward with her tin can, hoping against hope for the miracle to repeat itself. But today Mandira had not forgotten her purse, so she fumbled inside for some change. Having found some, she was about to drop it into the can, when a ten-rupee note slid into it. Astonished, she looked up.

It was Samir. Forlorn, lovesick, he had returned to that place too, since it was the spot that he had first met Mandira.

Mandira looked up. Her eyes met his. Both their anger melted away. They returned to the same restaurant for a reconciliatory cup of coffee ...

The day she got married, Mandira thought of the wise woman. What had her words really meant? She thought of her own desire to be the moth singeing her wings against the flame and blushed at her idiocy. Does anyone really want to suffer? And what was so wrong with her parents' life? Everyone had to get married. Unrequited love etc. was a pretty theme for poets and story writers. Who wanted to be romantic? One had to live in the real world.

So she began to live in the real world. Where flowers, wilted or otherwise, did not turn into gold coins nor discarded tissues into silk scarves.

But as the days sped past, many questions remained unanswered. Many quests remained unfulfilled. And when some strange centrifugal force began to spin Samir further and further away from her, she could not help wondering. Sometimes, she took out the silk scarf from the special box that she had placed it in as a memento of their first wonderful meeting, ran her hand over its soft surface, held it against her cheek and marvelled that something like that could have happened ... once upon a time.

And so their life went on. Having achieved one of the objectives of his life, namely Mandira, Samir went on to accomplish the next—which was success in his career.

And what did Mandira do in the meantime while he pursued his goal with the same single-minded persistence that he had pursued Mandira? She lived her life through his—it was enough of a goal for her. She haggled with vegetable vendors and saved his money, brought up his two children with the same commitment that she applied to everything she did. And—she guarded the silk scarf like a precious secret.

Then the day came that she opened the box and found that the scarf had mysteriously transmogrified into a crumpled piece of tissue. Shocked, she turned it over and over in her hand. She was positive, she knew that she had placed it there. Where could it have gone? Who could have taken it and placed a dirty, used tissue in its place? It was not precious, valuable enough for anyone to steal. It was precious only to her. An iron hand clutched her heart, squeezed it mercilessly. Her head spun around, she felt faint. Breathing heavily, she laid herself on her bed. Something told her that this boded no good.

Samir came home late that day. He was often late these days. In fact, lately they'd barely exchanged a few words each day and Mandira had been taking the scarf out more and more to look at it. That's why it gave her such a shock to find that it had turned into something so unexpected, so bizarre.

She sat up for him that night and in spite of his disinclination for conversation she told him about the missing scarf. He paled when he heard it. Something gripped his heart too. It was fear, mingled with guilt.

Something had happened. He knew what it was, in fact he could perhaps state the exact minute when the silk scarf went back to being the ordinary disposable object it originally was. He had been in bed with another woman at the time. But what could he tell Mandira? She would not believe him if he decided to tell her the story of the silk scarf now. And he certainly could not tell her why it had changed back.

The magical happening that he had been waiting for had occurred, but not in the way he would have liked it to.

'Are you sure you didn't keep it anywhere else?' he asked, falsely and glibly. Unfortunately, he had lived too and had come a long way from being the warm-hearted young man Mandira had first encountered. 'Check your cupboard thoroughly tomorrow.'

'I've checked it!' Mandira wailed.

'Check it again,' he said, turning his back. 'Mandira, I'm very tired, very sleepy.' He shrank away from her and lay sleepless for a long time. What, who was Mandira? If only he could part company from her. He couldn't stand the thought of these peculiar happenings. In any case the other woman attracted him much more now. But—but would, could Mandira take some kind of revenge? If not she, the magic that imbued their relationship might turn on him in some way. The thought chilled him and eventually prevented him from abandoning Mandira physically, though he had already cast her aside in his heart.

Mandira knew something momentous happened that day when the silk scarf vanished, never to return. The silken bond which had tied them together ... Samir turned more and more cold and distant. Their lives grew further and further apart. Was the wise woman's boon granted at last ... when she did not want it anymore? Too late she learned the lesson—that one should not cast words into the world without thinking. But oh, the brashness of lion-hearted youth. The prudence of old age shrivels up before its heat. One gains wisdom when it is too late to put it to any use.

The wise woman is too old now. She's senile, in fact. Mandira knows it's no use going to her. But she couldn't help thinking of what she had said … 'You can never have all the answers …' True, Samir could not supply her with the answer to the riddle of the silk scarf. Yet she had understood what it meant. That something precious had turned into dross. And hadn't she said she did not want any answers? That a question answered was like death? Was this, then, the end of it all?

The thought left her numb; as still and silent, inside and out, as a stone. It seemed horrifyingly strange that she should have known that day of her ignorant, restless youth, known what lay ahead of her. That she would receive what she had asked for.

Then she thought of the wilted flower that the wise woman had given her, the symbol of blighted love. How thoughtlessly she had dropped it into the beggar woman's tin can. But … the woman had been so grateful … so grateful …

Something drew her out of the house towards the spot where she had met the beggar woman and then Samir. It seemed a futile quest. The beggar woman would not be there after all those years. The place itself would have changed. And the wise woman had moved away. Yet she went.

She went and stood there and looked around. Yes, the place had changed. It looked more crowded, more prosperous, but dirtier. But the beggar woman was nowhere to be seen. Mandira waited, waited for a long time. She was turning away dispiritedly when a woman came running from somewhere and said, 'You, is it really you?'

She fell at Mandira's feet. Mandira was flabbergasted. Why was this dignified grey-haired woman doing that? Was she crazy?

'I owe it all to you!' the woman cried. 'Thanks to you, I don't have to beg any longer. I-I own that fruit stall.' She flung an energetic arm towards a kiosk in which apples flashed their rosy cheeks in tidy rows and oranges nestled next to them, round, complete and fragrant. Grapes and guavas kept them company, along with pomegranates and bananas.

An extraordinary thought made Mandira's heart leap. Could this be the beggar woman? No, no! Not possible.

'You must be mistaken,' she said, her voice faint. 'How could I be responsible?'

'I-I used to beg at that corner ...' she looked around and lowered her voice. 'You remember the gold coin, uh—the wilted flower that you changed into a gold coin with your amazing power?'

'The wilted flower that changed into a gold coin!' Goose pimples pinched Mandira's arms. Had she really accomplished that? But how? No wonder the beggar woman had been so grateful!

'I held on to it for some time,' the beggar woman continued. 'Since it was a magical thing. Then one day it occurred to me that even if it was magical, you must have given it to me for some purpose. Maybe you wanted me to stop begging. I sold it and started selling fruit. Little by little my business grew. Now I own 20 fruit stalls. But I continue to man this one personally. I have always lived in the hope that one day you will return ...'

Mandira sighed. Strange were the ways of fortune. But some things had to be clarified, credit given where it was due. 'I gave you a wilted flower,' she said. 'A wise woman had given it to me. It was her magic that turned it into a golden coin. Or maybe it was fate. I think … for me it was meant to be a wilted flower, for you a golden coin.'

'Perhaps,' the woman shrugged. 'Whatever it was, I received it from your hands, hence all my gratitude goes out to you,' the woman persisted.

She insisted on packing a huge basket of fruit for Mandira.

Mandira went home, marvelling at the wise woman's power. As she sat in her big empty house staring at the basket of fruit, suddenly something came to her. If the beggar woman could strive and multiply a gold coin into 20 fruit stalls surely she could manage some arithmetic of her own? Or was she perpetually doomed to possess useless objects like wilted flowers and crumpled tissues? On the other hand, though, hadn't she asked for them? Why oh why hadn't she listened to the wise woman?

However it was too late for regrets. So she lived on, in spite of Samir, in spite of the loss of the silk scarf.

But little did she guess why she could live on … guess that the foolish one had changed … she had acquired knowledge … in fact, she had become a wise woman herself. She had learnt that if you don't want answers you will not get any. And that actually you don't need any. Because life is for living … not just loving.

The Phalanx

Everything seemed to have come to a stop, all movement suspended. The water that had crept in, stealthy as a thief, to cover the hockey field five nights ago, was glassily still, asserting its presence like an intruder who has made up his mind to stay. The August air too had turned stagnant, trapping us in a sluggishness that made even the simple act of breathing an effort.

When it was first discovered that the floods had stolen in through our school gates, sealing us in and everything else out, we had been jubilant. How would the teachers arrive at school now? No classes. A holiday had fallen like manna from the heavens, along with the incessant rain that preceded the floods.

An attempt *was* made at first to confine us within our usual routine, to our outrage. The principal, Miss Nath, confronted the floods with her customary zeal, like any other challenge to her administrative power. It was a disruption that threatened that monument to her efficiency—the carefully organized and strictly enforced school timetable. How could she allow nature's wilfulness to prevail or give it undue importance? Indeed, when she announced the calamity at the rather depleted morning assembly, her tone was measured and discreet, as if she were handing out a list of duties for a school function. Perhaps it was to stave off the outbreak of mass hysteria she feared might result.

Her sagging cheeks were powdered more carefully than usual, her grey curls seemed cast in iron, and her bifocals had an implacable glint as she announced: 'Girls, we have no reason to be afraid. Everything is under control. We have enough provisions to feed you boarders for the next fifteen days.'

'Rotten potatoes,' Ruchika hissed from the side of her mouth. I hastily transformed my giggle into a burp, eliciting a sarcastic look from Anjali, who flanked me on the other side. Thankfully, being taller, we stood in one of the back rows. Despite the prospect of living on potatoes that tasted like sulphur-infused mud day in and day out, I was bounding upwards like an ebullient kite.

'Hope it rains and rains,' Ruchika went on as we filed into class. 'Hope we're marooned for the next one month.'

'Sure, and when they begin to feed us grass you'll be the happiest,' Kamini said. She was like that. A schoolgirl who refused to believe in ghosts and never touched the romantic novels we devoured.

'That won't happen. They airdrop food during floods. Packets of puris and laddoos.' Ruchika lived on hope. She was one of the few of us who meant it seriously when she prayed.

'And you honestly believe they'll be passed on to us? How'll Mrs Krishna maintain her blood sugar?' Simeran put in.

Mrs Krishna was the history teacher. One of our rare favourites. She had an endearing tendency to slump in her chair and mumble, 'I the-enk my blood sugar ees falling. Please spend the rest of the period ree-vising the last uh-chapter.' A guessing game we often played was trying to figure out Mr Krishna's identity, his occupation, age and physical appearance. She lived within the school premises and no one had ever laid eyes on him. Ruchika did claim that she had overheard Mrs Krishna talking to him on the phone, addressing him as 'darrling'. Her theory was that he was in the army, guarding the country on the front. Simeran, one of our army brats, hotly disputed it. Mrs Krishna was too sloppy to be an army wife, she maintained, in her crumpled cotton saris and rubber chappals and the strong scent of *Jabakusum* hair oil which sometimes insinuated itself into our exercise books after they were returned to us after a test. Apart from the fact that no one could believe she would address her husband as 'darling'. 'Ji' was more like it.

'I don't think it's going to be that much fun,' I volunteered, as the kite lost momentum unexpectedly and began to slide down to earth. 'We won't be able to share Naseem's lunch.' Naseem, a day scholar, brought the most delectable lunches of parathas and kebabs, to which we, as deprived boarders, often asserted our claim.

The thought was as dismaying as the prospect of staring at our books during the extended study hour that Miss Nath imposed on us in lieu of regular classes, where we sat revising chapters ad nauseam.

Providence, however, gave us a chance to celebrate eventually, when she decided in the whimsical way she had—again a corollary to her authority as principal—that it might be more beneficial for all to let us loose on the playground and follow our holiday routine.

When the announcement was made at morning assembly, we four were the most disorderly among the ragged mass of girls who rushed out yelling, oblivious of our status as students occupying the senior-most class, and as such expected to maintain a certain dignity. With the dormitories being on higher ground, far from the encroaching waters, the existence of the floods had so far been a mere whisper passed from ear to ear. Each exchanged rumour had whetted our curiosity to the point that nothing else mattered than that we should be the first to set eyes on this awesome phenomenon.

Within minutes we were clustered at the edge of the hockey field, gazing upon that placid lake with wonder.

'Do you think the water might rise further?' Simeran asked.

'It better not!' Kamini frowned virtuously at the prospect. 'We can't afford to miss more school. How will they complete the course?'

'Ugh ... don't be so boring,' Ruchika groaned. She picked up a stone and flung it into the water. It made a wonderfully defiant splash. The ripples spiralling out held us transfixed for a few moments, then we followed suit, even Kamini, raining such a volley of missiles to stir up the lazy waters that a teacher came and stopped us.

It became our new routine to saunter out to check the flood waters every morning after assembly and speculate on the level—

rising, falling or static? The shifting quality of this level opened up a host of anarchic possibilities, which we tossed around like a basketball.

And thus we entered the fifth day of the floods. It was a Wednesday, I recall, and I had woken up gloating over the prospect of another geography class missed. A mass of clouds spilled across the sky like cotton wool discarded from a dirty old mattress and the air congealed around us as thick as our breakfast porridge.

As I stood there gazing beyond the half-submerged gates at the sheet of water that covered the road in front of the school, water that stretched as far as my eye could reach, Ruchika muttered, 'Wonder how long it's going to last.' Something chopped at my tedium. It was the tone of her voice, scrubbed clean of even a glimmer of her earlier enthusiasm, weighted with a helpless resignation.

Something began to roil in my belly. A pea-sized ball of fear that sprang to life without any warning. Mortified, confused, I flung a quick look at Simeran. Her finely-shaped brows were bunched together and her teeth clamped on her full lower lip. I knew that expression. As my sly gaze travelled further, I noticed a similar anxiety reflected on Kamini's face. My fear bloated so rapidly that it began to press on my chest and interfere with my breathing.

Suddenly I yearned for the measured comfort, the safety of our daily routine, with each task occupying its allotted moment and nothing beyond it. The routine we had been so happy to toss away like a pair of worn-out shoes.

Simeran murmured, 'My aunt said boats are plying in the city, when she called.' She sounded weary.

'Why can't they send some here? We could go boating on the hockey field.' Kamini's feeble attempt at humour drew no response. We were squeezed dry, laughed out. Too many jokes had been told, too many possibilities explored. Nothing was left now but a stale ennui. Soon, I thought, we wouldn't even feel like talking.

I flung a despairing look at Ruchika. Her quick, eager face had congealed into a mask of boredom. In normal circumstances she would have topped the joke with a really funny one, had us in splits. Instead, she silently rubbed the sweat off her streaming face with a dirt-streaked handkerchief, making the long scar on her forehead stand out against her dark skin, then stretched her limbs and sighed.

'Fed up?' I asked. But Ruchika didn't reply. She stretched some more and sighed again, as if trying to blow off the heaviness. Her gaze swept away from the muddy water, which was beginning to stink, to traverse that stretch of playing field which was still dry, then halted.

Our eyes followed hers. A girl was walking down the field, a short, rather plump girl with a head of frizzy curls. She had a languorous, self-satisfied gait which I found offensive for some reason. How could anyone be so pleased with themselves at such a time? To complete the picture she raised a hand and waved, in the style of a film star acknowledging the applause of an adoring crowd. I was about to make a derisive remark when Ruchika sprang up, mumbling something unintelligible.

We watched as she loped across the scrubby grass with an easy grace. 'What does she want with Ruby?' Kamini asked.

Simeran shrugged. I watched as Ruchika came to a standstill and the two of them began to stroll off towards the shady verandah that bordered the middle school classrooms, the tall slender figure and the short plump one. It would have been comical but for the harmony their postures exuded.

'It's too hot, yaar,' I whined, standing up. 'Let's go inside.' The others rose silently but I could see my own bewilderment mirrored in their eyes.

We had never had much to do with Ruby. She was one of those girls who, though they were older than us, were compelled to remain in a junior class for obvious reasons. Other than exchanging a chance remark when I came across her in the dressing room, often shaving her legs (she was particular about her appearance), there had never been much interaction with her. On one occasion, I recalled, she had offered to do my hair. She was good at things like that.

Ruchika had, however, never been interested in dressing up, even on a Saturday when the brothers from the boys' school visited their sisters and a rare opportunity to attract male attention presented itself. The possibility of having a boyfriend, exchanging love notes, an activity more romantically real than mooning after film stars, did not seem to excite her. So what did she want with Ruby?

That evening we were told that the floods were beginning to recede and it was hoped that life would return to normal the next day. We greeted the news with cheers as exuberant as those with which we had welcomed their coming.

During the study hour after dinner, we hung over our books with a fierce concentration, instead of surreptitiously passing notes to each other or doodling in the margins of our books, the way we had been doing the last few days. It was our final year of school, the dreaded board exams were barely four months away and the pressure to perform suddenly came back into alarming focus.

Determinedly, I stayed up with the others, studying into the late hours even though my eyes were beginning to droop with weariness and my mind refused to register facts that crawled like plaguing ants across the white pages of my book. I couldn't ignore the uneasy truth thrumming inside me like a discordant sitar—we had lost five precious days to the floods. I couldn't let down my parents. I had to produce the brilliant results they expected.

A sound as loud as a pistol shot made me start. Ruchika had snapped her book shut. Her heavy-lidded eyes met my questioning ones defiantly. 'Oh, what's the bloody use?' she said, 'I'm going to fail in any case.'

She stood up. 'Good night, girlies, happy studying.' She waved indifferently and walked away.

We were too astonished to react. It was Anjali, whose ferocity on the hockey field made us keep a wary distance from her, who said with a low snigger, 'Looks like she actually wants to fail.'

'Why should she want to fail?' Simeran shot back, affronted. The four of us formed a solid phalanx. An attack on any one of us was an attack on all.

'Why shouldn't she?' Anjali's smile had a slimy edge, a knowingness that made my skin tighten.

'Stop talking rot! No one wants to fail.'

'And Ruchika's not such an ass,' Kamini added.

'Some people do,' Anjali said. 'And please don't disturb me. *I* want to study. *I* don't want to fail.'

I kept up the pretence of staring at my book as long as I could. But when I couldn't stand it any longer, I got up too. Ignoring the questioning gazes clustering around me, I said good night like a stranger and trudged up the dimly lit stairs to bed.

'Damn!' Simeran turned, taking me by surprise. In order to save time, we were sharing the same cubicle to bathe. For modesty's sake we had turned our backs to each other as we prepared to dip water over our naked bodies out of the dingy metal buckets the school provided us with. Modesty was still at a premium in the sixties. There were girls who came to school with their bodies concealed within burkhas. And even the thought of setting eyes on one another's uncovered form would have embarrassed us beyond measure, even though expediency sometimes compelled us to share a bathing cubicle.

'I've started too,' she said, holding out a stained panty. I stopped in the middle of unbuttoning my white blouse. Simeran was the one late starter amongst us; she hadn't begun to menstruate as yet, even though she'd turned sixteen this July. She had never been sure whether to be pleased, or anxious like her mother was.

Now that it had finally happened, she looked completely unnerved. So unnerved that she had forgotten to cover herself with a towel, leaving the curve of a small, pale breast visible in silhouette to my shocked gaze.

I averted my eyes hurriedly. 'You-you can borrow some pads from me,' I said.

Later I realized that I should have offered some words of reassurance, some comfort at that traumatic moment. But I was so flustered that all I could think of was getting dressed again and running out of the cubicle.

'So, you've joined the world of adults at last,' Kamini laughed. 'Welcome, my dear!'

Simeran said nothing. She looked bemused, as if still unable to grasp what had happened. I could understand. Hadn't we all experienced it? Even knowing it was inevitable was not enough to prepare you for the bombshell, that something like that could actually overtake you. That for some unfathomable reason you were condemned to bleed every month for a good portion of your life.

We were seated at the dinner table. The news had already insinuated itself into many curious ears, been greeted with interest particularly because Simeran's situation had aroused much speculation. We often discussed the awful implications of such a landmark event passing her by altogether, discreetly, of course, in her absence. Whatever people had heard of such complications, which had beset distant relatives sometimes, or acquaintances of acquaintances, had been dredged up and shared, accompanied with exclamations of dismay that our Simeran might be subjected to such trauma. Hence the relief, the jubilation. If it had been acceptable, we might even have asked her to celebrate with a treat at the canteen. But all we could do was proffer congratulations and as more experienced folks, some half-baked advice.

'You can get pregnant now,' was Anjali's contribution. 'You better stay far from boys.'

'Shut up!' Simeran suddenly came alive from her stupor. 'Stop saying disgusting things.'

'I'm only warning you for your own good,' Anjali replied with mock gravitas. 'A beauty like you needs to be careful. Men could easily lose control around you.'

'So we have great chances of getting pregnant here,' I said quickly. Simeran looked ready to throw the contents of her plate at Anjali. 'We meet boys all the time, don't we?'

Maybe I should have let her, I thought, the very next moment. Doesn't Anjali deserve it, the jealous bitch?

'You can get pregnant only when you get married.' The small fluty voice had the confidence of incomplete knowledge. It was Nimmi, little Nimmi from class five. What was she doing on our side of the table, sitting in Ruchika's place? Our preoccupation with Simeran's extraordinary news had made us overlook the fact. 'When a man and woman sleep together in the same bed.'

'And God puts a baby into the woman's belly,' Anjali added. The laughter was loud enough to bring the teacher in charge scurrying to our table.

'How did that silly Nimmi change places with Ruchika?' Simeran whispered fiercely as we strode to the study hall.

'Ruchika must have asked her,' I muttered, a coiled snake hardening in my belly.

Simeran didn't reply but her face darkened.

It was Kamini who surprised us by hissing, 'That bitch Ruby.' The venom in her voice made my skin shrivel. Even more so because it was spurting up inside me too.

'Why did you start sitting here, child?' Anjali asked Nimmi at breakfast the next day. Her tone was gallingly syrupy.

'Ruchika asked me to change.' Nimmi's large eyes were wary, her voice muffled by a mouthful of egg and toast.

'I suppose she wanted to sit next to Ruby.' Anjali's eyes had a derisive glint as they met mine.

'Why not she? There's no rule that you can't change seats.' Simeran tried to shrug it off.

'Of course,' Anjali's voice was bland. 'You can sit next to whoever you like. But, I always believed you four were inseparable.'

Kamini kicked me under the table. 'So what? Just because we're friends it doesn't mean we have to cling to each other all the time,' she said. 'In any case we're going to leave school soon. What do you think will happen then? We won't be inseparable any longer.'

It was a brave attempt. But not effective enough. It did not vanquish the smirk that was twisting Anjali's thin lips or the embarrassed looks on the other girls' faces as they glanced away.

Despite everything, I couldn't help sneaking a look at Ruchika, seated at the far end of the long table. Her mouth was curving into a tender smile as she spooned pickle onto Ruby's plate. She looked … besotted.

An invisible tattoo needle began to dance on my skin and the custard turned sour on my tongue. Had Ruchika and I really been the best of friends for the last six years?

'That bitch, Ruby!' Simeran spat as we sat on the steps at the edge of the hockey field.

The ground had long since dried out and the floods were a distant and faint memory. Other matters occupied our minds now—the coming exams and the thought that after they were over we would be flung apart. A thought we did not want to contemplate too much right now. We were still trying to figure out the mystery of Ruchika's defection.

'Why blame Ruby?' Kamini said. 'It's Ruchika's fault too.'

This kind of logic always drove me mad. 'It's more Ruby's fault,' I said stubbornly. 'She was the one always trying to suck up to her.'

'No,' Simeran astonished me. 'It's Ruchika's fault too. If she was a true friend she wouldn't have ditched us like that.'

'What's the point of working ourselves up?' Kamini said. 'She's not going to come back to us.'

'I don't want her to come back,' I burst out. It was a relief to say that finally. 'I wouldn't want to be friends with her now … after all this …'

Kamini looked frightened. Her mouth opened as if she wanted to stop me from saying what I was going to. It was too late. 'Do you know what they're saying? That ...' But when it came to the crunch, words failed me too.

I watched the flush spreading over Simeran's face, visible despite the thickening light. I watched Kamini's chest rise and fall rapidly, oblivious to the monotonous humming of the mosquitoes above my head, the burning jab of their stings. The shouts of the girls from the basketball court belonged to another world. It was only when the dinner bell set up an insistent clangour did we start up and begin to trudge mechanically towards the dining hall.

The evening air had a slight nip now and the smoky scent of winter was growing stronger day by day. I slid into my place at the dining table and contemplated the meal served out in my plate. Two round potatoes swimming in an indefinite-coloured gravy, pale cauliflower squashed almost beyond recognition and tired looking chapattis on the side. An overwhelming sense of relief wrapped around me like a cosy blanket. In a couple of months I would be far from this place. It was such a warm relief that the sound of someone sniggering across the table almost escaped me.

'What did you say?' Simeran's voice was like a knife.

'Do you really want to know?' There was such malevolence in Anjali's smile that I almost reached out and placed a restraining hand on Simeran's arm. But an unexpected fear prevented me. Could we dare, or rather bear to touch each other again, however innocently? I thought of the numerous occasions when I had sat, carelessly holding Ruchika's hand. The comfort of that warm, dry touch ...

'Of course I do!' I didn't know about the others, but there was something I wished to convey. Ruchika was no longer one of us and Anjali had better realize it, sooner rather than later.

'Tell them Nimmi.'

Nimmi reddened. Her eyes dropped. 'Don't be scared. Tell them ... you know,' Anjali went on cheerfully, 'Little Nimmi was asking me if two girls can have babies if they sleep in the same bed.'

No one laughed this time. 'Please pass the water,' I said. 'This conversation is becoming boring. I didn't know people could be so stupid.' I couldn't even feel sorry for Nimmi, when I saw tears spring up in her eyes.

It was lucky perhaps that Ruby didn't play hockey. Because I would have hit out at her shins with all the force my hatred could produce. Not a trifling amount, as Anjali's howl of pain testified. It did not give me the kind of pleasure hitting Ruby would have, but was satisfying all the same. More because of the fear I saw leap up in her eyes.

'Good for you,' Simeran said later. But my smile remained meagre, because there is a kind of pleasure that festers inside you secretly, does not permit you to laugh aloud, lest others get wind of it.

The first star struggled to become visible despite the glow of the city lights, and the trees at the far edge of the field were like ominous black cut-outs against the reddish sky. An occasional vehicle crept past the gates, its headlights fending off the growing darkness with luminous arms. 'What do they actually do inside the razai?' I asked, abandoning all remnants of constraint. 'I mean two girls can't do the same things, uh—boys and girls can.'

'They kiss each other, you know, like in the movies,' Anjali's grin no longer seemed repulsive.

She had become a reluctantly accepted sympathizer now. All we knew was that it was becoming more and more unbearable to see the two of them mooning around. This shamelessness was an affront, as outrageous as sleeping in the same bed. The worst was that Ruchika didn't seem to understand what she had done. She greeted us in the same cheery tone, oblivious to our icy responses. Insensible to the fact that she had broken the phalanx, exposing us to the mockery of the world. We had become quite clear about one thing now—anyone who was against them was with us.

'Yech!' Simeran pretended to retch. 'Do girls enjoy kissing each other ... like that?'

Suddenly I thought, if Ruchika had been here she'd have laughed and said, 'Want to try? A French kiss?' I shook the thought out of my head, aghast that it could dare to creep in. But it wouldn't go away. It grew into an image of Ruchika loudly kissing her hand. 'Want to kiss like this? Like this, like this?'

Had that conversation ever taken place?

A wind was beginning to spring up, rustling the leaves of the trees, numbing the tips of my fingers.

'They do,' Anjali went on. Her voice went low, even though there was no one around for yards. 'I believe they suck each other's boobs ... and other things. People have heard them.'

'What nonsense! Kissing is possible. But ... No! I refuse to believe it!' Kamini was as unyielding as she ever had been.

I'm not sure if the seeds of the plan were planted then, the same way I'm not sure when it was formulated. Anjali played a leading role and so did Simeran and I. But I'm also not sure if Kamini was as reluctant to follow it through as she appeared then.

When it took final shape, the plan seemed perfect. It would accomplish both our goals, though at that time curiosity seemed more in the forefront than their disgrace. And it would be a fitting finale to our tenure in school, because we scheduled it for the last night.

The floor was as cold as only a cement floor could be on a December night. But I didn't mind crawling across it on my belly—I took an insane delight in it, a delight quite different from the one that accompanied the other schoolgirl pranks we had indulged in. Only, this time Ruchika was on the other side. And Anjali was my counterpart, crossing the floor from the other end of the dormitory, negotiating her way under the sea of beds. The moment we reached their bed we would give the signal, two loud coughs. Simeran would turn on the lights and we would fling the quilt off.

And we would find out what they did inside it.

The last assembly in school remains a blur in my mind. No doubt there were lectures and exhortations and much advice on how to conduct ourselves in the big bad world outside, which was waiting to devour little morsels like us. The school song was rendered with much gusto, I suppose, along with the usual hymns. We had been part of many such assemblies—the only difference was that this was *our* special one. All I recall is the struggle to keep my eyes open throughout and later, the farewells as we set off with our tin trunks and bedding rolls, along with the parents and relatives who had come to collect us. We were too dazed perhaps to feel the pain of parting, and the significance of this departure. Or the thought of the real world waiting outside these walls had such a strong pull that it obscured any other emotion. I do recall the ice of embarrassment overlaying the outwardly sentimental goodbyes, and the fact that our hugs were not as effusive and heartfelt as they always were when we went home for the holidays. Even the exhortations to write seemed mechanical.

Perhaps that moment was too deeply embedded in our minds. That moment of baffling, corrosive knowledge. Before Ruby's shrill screams, mingled with Ruchika's deeper ones, deafened us.

Sometimes I think ... maybe it would have been better if we hadn't tried to find out. Because some things are better left hidden beneath a quilt. And then ... as they had tearfully declared, what's wrong with two girls loving one another?

That was a long time ago. I was a child then, a child who had no way of judging what kind of love was right and what was wrong.

Closure

The day was packing itself up as tidily as a salesman who had sold enough of his wares to be totally satisfied. The evening cup of tea had been just right, Amma thought—flavoursome without the acrid taste of over-brewed leaves. The biscuits that accompanied it had felt crisp and fresh beneath her teeth and the namkin was the way she liked it—mildly spicy.

And now the sun was gathering up its brilliant robes, slipping beneath the high-rises, leaving a faint evanescence behind. Even as Amma watched this luminous exit, darkness moved in, so swiftly that it enclosed her before she realized that the distinct landscape of the city was just a vista of shadowy shapes now. She was savouring the moment, letting the cloak of invisibility wrap around her, letting herself dissolve into it, when the maid, Mamta, bustled in and switched on the light with an officious click.

'Why do you sit in the dark, Ammaji?' she scolded.

As usual, Amma masked her irritation with facetiousness. 'To save electricity,' she said. It was the only way to cope with Mamta's earnestness. What made it more enjoyable was the fact that though Mamta did throw her a suspicious glance once in a while, Amma was positive that each busy cell in the girl's body staunchly believed that someone as old as Amma couldn't crack jokes.

'Save electricity?' Mamta's shapely eyebrows (made possible through Amma's largesse) arched up. 'Ammaji, don't you know how much your son and daughter-in-law earn?'

'How much?' Amma asked innocently.

But Mamta avoided this trap. She wrapped her sari *pallu* around her waist with an efficient air and said, 'If you don't know—how would I, a mere servant, know?'

Amma squeezed the budding smile back into her mouth. She knew what an accomplished eavesdropper Mamta was. She'd come upon her several times, poised against Samar and Manisha's bedroom door, as if she'd halted in the act of knocking. Not that Amma blamed her too much. Knowledge was power, wasn't it? And who needed it more than a servant girl?

'All right, Ammaji,' Mamta went on. 'What should I cook today? You know they're out for dinner—they will go there straight from office.'

Out for dinner ... suddenly Amma was overcome with an immense exhaustion. She had made too many such decisions in her life, and the thought of one more capsized the boat of her composure without warning.

'Cook whatever you want,' she said. 'I'm going out too.'

'Ammaji!' Mamta's fine brows would have disappeared into her hair if the doorbell hadn't rung just then.

Amma shook her head, the way one jiggles a dysfunctional appliance to force it to work. What possessed her to say that?

Mamta returned, looking mystified, no, troubled, and handed Amma a note. Amma gazed at it for a long while, her breath coming with a deliberate evenness, while her face remained blank, then rose purposefully. 'Tell him I'm coming in a moment,' she said, her voice unusually crisp.

She stood before the mirror for a while, examining herself. Not too bad for seventy-five, she thought inconsequentially, trying to smother the violent churning inside her. Strange, how things happen when you least expect them. Even when you've been waiting for them to happen. Jerkily, she ran a comb through her short, grey hair. Manisha had suggested this style, being least troublesome, and Amma hadn't resisted too much. Sometimes it was better to drift along with the dominant current, and not waste energy that was becoming more precious as it became scarce. And what did it matter what her hair looked like? Her mouth could have done with a touch of lipstick, she thought. She always tried to look good, not out of vanity but rather to present a pleasant sight to the viewer. She was reaching for the lone tube on her dressing table when Mamta's wide-eyed face loomed beside her in the mirror. Amma frowned. Fond as she was of her, the girl became too familiar at times.

'Mamta,' she said, emphasizing each word so that there should be no misunderstanding, 'Take that suitcase into the car.'

'Ammaji!' Mamta's clear voice quavered like an agitated sitar. 'When did you pack that? Where-why are you going?'

Amma chose not to reply to that, though she could have said that she was free to go whenever and wherever she wished. She could have also told Mamta about the parable of the wise virgins in the Bible but it wouldn't have made much sense to the girl. How would she know how important it was to always be ready?

Mamta made a last frantic attempt. 'Please, let-let me call them!'

'Let them be! Just carry the suitcase to the car.' Amma's voice was harsh.

Mamta fell apart then. 'Please don't go, Ammaji,' she wept. 'Please! Forgive my impertinence, haven't I looked after you the best way I could?'

Amma softened a bit. 'It's not your fault, child,' she said. 'And now I have to go.'

She was very conscious of Mamta's trembling form half dragging the large suitcase to the car. She could forgive her for her smugness now, the thoughtless arrogance of her youth. Mamta looked even more stricken as the driver opened the door for Amma. Her mouth opened as if to say something as she clutched Amma's hands in farewell, then it closed again helplessly.

It was only when they were some distance from the house that Amma began to feel sorry for Mamta, remembering the sweat pearling down her smooth dark face, the pain in her baffled eyes. In her own way she had tried to be good to Amma. No, Amma really had no complaints, but of course, she could not satisfy everyone's curiosity. And then, she herself didn't know where she was going, only that it was a summons that she could not refuse.

She thought of the chain of events this simple action might unfold. Perhaps Mamta was already on the phone sobbing out the news. Perhaps Samar and Manisha were already driving home—

their party interrupted, their so-essential networking abandoned halfway. Perhaps Manisha was thinking, 'Trust Amma to do something like this. Interrupt an important evening.' Perhaps Samar was thinking, 'Oh God, did she have to leave like this?'

Conversely, Mamta might already be ransacking the room, going through the drawers, looking for neglected valuables. Amma wondered if she was capable of it. The eavesdropping made her think she could be. Well, she would be rewarded if she were. Amma had abandoned the old gold bangle, the one she had intended to give Stuti, her granddaughter, in the left hand drawer of her dressing table. Sometimes it gave her pleasure to be whimsical, leave it to destiny to decide who would receive what, whether they deserved it or not, rather than follow convention. And she had never been sure who had a better right to it, Stuti because of the ties of blood or Mamta for services rendered. Mamta's snoopiness made her confident she could walk away with the prize. Stuti, who had grown distant both in terms of space and time, was in any case not around to claim it.

The car negotiated the crowded streets with a sedate briskness and now it was crossing the bridge. She glimpsed what looked like a row of low hills on the other side and then the darkness vanished as suddenly as it had inundated her that evening. But it was not Mamta who switched on the light here. Amma felt confused. Was it already dawn?

The car slowed down, stopped. 'We have arrived, madam,' said the driver gravely, opening the door.

Amma stepped out, stretched and tidied the folds of her sari before entering the gate that emerged before her. She wasn't sure what she felt at that moment. Closing one door to open another. Would she miss Samar, Manisha, Stuti, Mamta and so all the other people she had left behind—or they her? Perhaps.

But closures took place all the time, didn't they? One climbed the ladder, leaving one rung behind to stand on another. We all get used to it, she thought, it doesn't really matter now.

The Path

They did not seek the path—it found them. Maze-like, it led them on such a meandering journey that try as they might, it was impossible to calculate the distance they had covered. Even the roughest estimate eluded them. The passage of time remained the only certainty as they kept track of the phases of the moon—dark, bright, dark—and bright again now. That and the fact that all the myths they had employed to keep hope alive were on the verge of extinction.

'We're trapped,' Bhanmal said, his breath forcing itself out in jagged gasps as he collapsed onto the large rock that jutted out of the mountainside. 'This road is a whirlpool, sucking us in deeper and deeper. I fear ... our wanderings will never cease.'

Lalchand remained silent. Bhanmal's complaints no longer affected him, not even the sobbing note at the end of the old man's tirade.

He gazed down into the trough that ploughed such a deep furrow between the hills. This land fascinated him, with its steep inclines, strange trees and meadows greener than any he had seen. Would it turn out to be their final destination? They had tried to get off the road so many times, only to be driven back on to it again.

Behind him, Kishan came up with a riposte.'A *bhanwar* sucks you down, Bhanmalji, this road has led us upward.'

Lalchand could imagine his red mouth twitching, the sly, mocking glance he would fling at the others. The journey had leached out so many of the courtesies that had once been an integral part of their being. Thrashed them out rather, the way grain is removed, leaving just the husk. Were they that? Just the husks of what were once complete human beings? A ripple of unease pinched his arms, wiping out the euphoria the landscape had brought. An even more ominous thought followed. What if there was no final destination? What if this endless journey was their punishment for abandoning their code?

'And it's not a road—just our bewildered, exhausted feet carrying us anywhere they can find a foothold,' Jairaj hissed through his teeth. The harsh crack of a twig snapping followed and Lalchand had to glance back, despite himself, and respond.

'Why blame the road or our feet? At least they've carried us so far. Kept us alive.'

'Alive for what?' Jairaj viciously flung the two parts of the twig on the ground.

'We should save the wood for our cooking fire,' Lalchand said, his eyes as chilly as the evening breeze in these mountains.

'There's plenty of wood. And what are you planning to cook?' Jairaj jeered.

The question was answered right away. Through the humming sound of an arrow, and as their heads swung in that direction, they discovered a fat hare neatly pinned on the ground.

Kishan sucked in his breath quickly. 'How do you manage to see them?' His eyes were like wide gashes in his face, with fear leaking out of them.

Nathu, to whom this question was addressed, simply shrugged and walked soundlessly towards the slain animal. With practiced ease he extracted the precious arrow for future use.

Lalchand ignored Bhanmal's almost demented muttering, 'At least those skills are keeping us alive.'

Soon the rabbit had been skinned and was roasting over a fire. The herbs springing up from the earth all around them had an enticing fragrance, however, they were wary of using them to flavour their food. The salt and chilly mixture they had bought at the last village did well enough. Who knew what unknown poisons lurked in these mysterious plants?

The hare was not that large but was enough for them, enough for the spare repasts they had gotten accustomed to. The fullness in his belly brought such languor that Lalchand was tempted to stretch out on the ground and let the breeze stroke his face.

Kishan, a fast eater, was already rubbing his hands clean with mud when Nathu remarked, his grey-green eyes fixed on a distant point in the valley. 'Are those houses?' He pointed a long finger to the end of the gorge.

'Houses?' Lalchand shaded his eyes against the midday sun. Its rays flashed briefly on the flat stones of a roof. Soon, outlines of the small stone structures began to emerge—the houses that had become familiar to them, so different from the flat-roofed dwellings of their native land.

'Shall we head there?' Kishan passed his tongue over his dry, chapped lips. 'There might be proper food, rotis ...'

'Maybe, it is meant to be our final destination.' Bhanmal's cloudy eyes sparked with hope.

'And maybe there'll be stones to drive us away,' Jairaj snorted.

'Surviving you has been harder than surviving the Afghans,' Kishan shot back. 'Let's take our chance. It was only once that we were driven away with stones.'

'Why not?' Lalchand said.

'I say we do,' Bhanmal's voice showed more resolve than it had for a long, long time. 'When will we stop wandering?'

'When our feet tell us to!' Kishan's gap-toothed grin marred the perfection of his features.

'And if they don't? I say if we do decide to stay, we should dig in and not let anyone drive us out,' Jairaj glared. 'Not our feet, nor the villagers.'

'When we wanted to stop at the last village you didn't let us,' Kishan's nostrils flared.

'Ha, you wanted to stay there because of the girl. We wouldn't have lasted long. I saved you from being beaten up,' Jairaj snarled.

'Ummm ... that place wasn't right,' Nathu murmured.

'He will decide for us, the half-wit,' Jairaj hissed under his breath.

'Hasn't he just fed you?' Kishan cried.

'Enough!' Lalchand held up a hand. 'We'll see what awaits us there.'

'I had a wonderful dream last night,' Nathu began. 'I was in Rai Pithora's palace ...'

'Shall we move on?' Jairaj interrupted roughly. 'I don't dream of palaces but I would like to sleep under a proper roof tonight. These blankets are not enough protection against the dew.'

'Be thankful you have something,' Kishan frowned.

'We have much to be thankful for,' Bhanmal said, his voice so low that a gust of wind almost blew his words away. He rose wearily. 'Leave me there at least, if you all cannot stay. I can't travel any further. Surely they'll take pity on an old man?'

'Who knows?' Jairaj said cruelly. He rose and sent a bone whirling into the air. 'I still wish I had perished on the battlefield.'

No one responded to that, only Kishan's mouth drew down in a sneer. They had tossed around that question among them so many times that sometimes it felt it had lost all meaning, become merely rhetorical. Why doesn't he let go, Lalchand thought, as he turned his steps downhill towards the village. But despite his irritation, he knew that it lurked somewhere within each of them, had plunged its roots as deep as an addiction that cannot be cured.

The memory still made him shiver. His moment of decision. There had been no time for deliberation—what was to be done had to be done in the blinking of an eyelid. Stand and face the onslaught till you were mowed down, or run and save your life. It was more like a reflex, the impulse that made him abandon his warrior's conceit and wheel his horse around to gallop away from the battlefield. The mlecchas' systematic onslaught had reached the point when even an eternal optimist like him had to abandon hope. All around him, men were toppling like felled trees. He had seen Chandan's sword flash in the dimming light as he lunged at an Afghan. He was about to call out to his friend, when an arrow spiralled out of nowhere to pierce Chandan's eye. Imprisoned in the horror of that moment, Lalchand could only gaze helplessly at that beloved, robust frame sliding off the horse. And before his paralyzed arms could reach out to save his friend, the Afghan had hacked Chandan's head off with one savage blow.

His cry of grief had plunged down his throat instead of out. Gasping, shuddering, gagging with horror, he had let his horse bear him away from the testing ground. A failure. A traitor. But that remorseless logic was bloating inside him so rapidly that the stout fortress of his conditioning collapsed like a straw hut. What was it worth, it argued—adding his corpse to the bloody pile, that stinking harvest of human debris? Wiping himself out like Chandan had, in a war that was already lost.

At twenty-six he was the veteran of numerous battles, had stood proudly on this very field a year ago, chasing this same enemy. He had experienced his share of carnage, was participating in it as enthusiastically as his adversary till just moments ago—in the business of bloodletting and hacking of limbs. But at that particular moment all he had wanted was to get away from the shrieks of the dying and wounded, the women's desperate wails, the trumpeting of maddened elephants, the neighing of agitated horses and, the Afghans' ominous war cries—already intoxicated with the prospect of victory.

How much can change in a year, or rather in just a few hours.

He had let his horse choose the path. Men were scatering in all directions, calling out to others to join them. 'To the town!' some cried. 'To Tarain!' Who was he to follow?

The deluge of arrows still rained incessantly. Neighing frantically, his horse had borne him further and further away, but it was only when he had reached the ends of the killing field that he picked up the parallel sound of hoofs pounding alongside, heard someone panting fearfully next to him.

The aristocratic Bhanmal.

'Son, son, where shall we go?'

'Just keep going, ji!'

They had chanced on the other three at the first village they stopped at—a negligible cluster of mud dwellings. How often had he ridden past such hamlets without a second glance, never dreaming that some day he would gaze at one with the yearning of a parched man in the desert?

Fear had taken such deep root in their hearts that for a few moments, they had hesitated, despite their overpowering need for sanctuary. Only the sight of three other horses tied to a tree gave them the courage to proceed. In the courtyard of the first house a hulking form, still encased in armour, loomed through the greyness—Jairaj, an almost giant. Kishan, whose flying curls made him look foppish even in his battle array, was having his wounds dressed. An old woman was slapping turmeric paste onto the gashes on his legs and arms. It was only later that Lalchand noticed that he had lost some teeth too.

'A spear in my face,' he'd said with a wry grin.

They were all battered, slashed in some part of the body or the other, despite their armour. All expect Nathu.

The small, lithe boy—at first sight that's what he'd looked like to Lalchand—had come forward to help Bhanmal remove his *bajuband*. The evening murk had camouflaged the faint lines around his eyes that became evident the next day.

'So the battle went against us?' The elderly man whose white eyebrows jutted out like a thatch over his sunken eyes, stated, rather than asked, as he offered them a lota of water.

Bhanmal had nodded, while Lalchand simply looked away.

They had been too drained, too demoralized by the day's events to speak much. Silently they accepted the rotis that a young woman slapped out at one end of the courtyard. The clang of the tawa, the repetitive sound of rotis being shaped felt unreal. Overcome by an embarrassing hunger, they had chewed mechanically, then indicated their gratitude in hushed tones. As the darkness became more complete, the silence began to press against Lalchand's ears, fresh from the memory of war's cacophony. Stretched out on the coarse straw mats the man had apologetically provided, huddled under the tattered covering that smelt of the cowshed, all he wanted was to sleep, to shut out the images still clamouring in his mind. But sleep had been a tease, giving itself in niggard morsels. It was not just the mid-January cold—the balls of cow dung smouldering near them provided only an impression of heat. He had started awake over and over again to escape the torment of his dreams. Beside him Bhanmal twitched and moaned, pounded his heels on the ground. Jairaj's shouts had jerked him awake once. '*Maro*! *Maro*!' he had yelled. Only Kishan and Nathu seemed to sleep without a care.

The sky was still a powdery charcoal-grey when he heard his hosts stirring. Someone was coaxing flames from a fire, another intoning a prayer. Farmers rose early to attend to their fields, he had heard.

It soon became clear that crops were the last things on their hosts' minds. In between offering a frugal breakfast of milk and parched gram to their guests, they were busy gathering their few belongings together. A dhoti, an *angarkha*, a blanket, some utensils, bundles of provisions. Fodder for the animals.

He had not been able to collect his thoughts sufficiently yet to decide what he should do next. Head homeward towards Dilli? Try his luck at the town of Tarain to regroup with others like him who might have survived? He had still believed those were valid options.

'Are you going on a journey?' Jairaj had asked the old man after a while.

He had folded his hands, adopted that deferential half-bowing posture he'd adopted towards them ever since they arrived. 'It's time to move to a safer place, ji. Now that the battle has been lost, the Afghans will spare no one in the area around Tarain. The town people may be able to buy their lives, but what have we to offer? Better to leave before they find us.' He had gazed at them for a few moments, then continued, examining his hands. 'If a humble man like me can offer some advice, ji, they will be on the lookout for runaway soldiers too. You need to put some distance between yourself and them.'

Runaway. The word jolted Lalchand out of his stupor and rang in his ears. *Bhagora.*

While he was quite conscious of what he had done, in that desperate moment of decision the shame of that epithet had retreated to some remote, inaccessible crevice of his brain. *Bhagora.* Nausea uncurled like a slimy worm inside him. Had he lost his senses in the instant that he shelved his dharma? The knowledge hammered his head—all his earlier feats of valour were as nothing now, their glory lost as inexorably as Chandan's life. How could he have thought of returning home?

In a flash of distasteful insight he witnessed the same notion mirrored in the others' faces—Bhanmal twisting the numerous rings on his knotty fingers over and over again; Jairaj's frown burrowing deeper into his forehead as his gaze dug into the courtyard floor; Kishan tugging at the ends of his moustache as if he wanted to tear it out. Only Nathu simply let out a soft, sibilant sigh.

A desperate thought ripped through his mind—should they return to Tarain, seek out an opportunity to retrieve what fragments of honour they could?

Bhanmal's measured, courtly tones interrupted his flow of thought. 'My sons, having retreated from the battlefield to save our lives it would be wiser to continue on the same course.' At that time, being the eldest, still imbued with the aura of authority, he had taken the decisions. They had deferred to him without dispute, even the contrary Jairaj. 'Once the Afghanis have filled their bellies, they will return to their barbarous lands. We can go back then, to rally around our leaders, reclaim our lands and the familiar pattern of our lives.'

Bhanmal's grave, deep voice, the dignity his clipped grey beard endowed him with, his almost poetic words, reassured them. With a few sentences, he had buried the indignity of the word *bhagora*.

The old villager was a rustic, his vocabulary limited. They had been prudent. True valour did not mean throwing your life away, but saving it for another battle. For the welfare of your own. They would return, pick up the scattered threads of their existence, weave the old design into them again. A vision of his family reared up—his aged father, pulling at his hookah. His mother—ensconced in her prayer room. His wife Nandkunwari—her pert, dark-skinned face with its sideways smile. His two laughing, leaping boys. His two-year-old daughter, forever clamouring for a perch on his shoulder. How thankful he was that he had left his family in Dilli instead of transporting them to the field like many did—even the king. He had been foresighted enough to spare them that horror.

He could see Kishan's face brightening; the clouds seemed to flee from Jairaj's taut brow too. Only Nathu remained inscrutable.

'We should leave this place,' he added simply, startling them, as if he'd read some ill omen into it. It was the first time they had heard his voice. It had a high-pitched somewhat brassy resonance that compelled you to dwell on his words.

The villagers were piling their possessions into their bullock carts, women were clambering in, pulling up children, tucking them into their laps. As they rose, he could not help registering the thought that they, who had possessed so much in their real lives, had nothing to carry but themselves—and of course, their weapons.

At that instant, his gaze propelled itself to the armour they had discarded last night.

He was not the only one contemplating it.

'I beg you, kind sirs,' the old man folded his hands again. 'Please remove it. If the mlecchas come and find it here, they may demolish our poor dwellings completely ... There-there is a blind well on the outskirts of the village. You can throw it in there. Maybe ... recover it later.'

'That is a wise suggestion, my good man,' Bhanmal nodded.

But as they flung those metal casings that had carapaced their vulnerable frames so effectively into the well, Lalchand experienced a ripple of unease. As if the warrior part of him was being sloughed off, consigned to a bottomless pit. The uncomfortable thought returned like a niggling ache—how much of his essential self had he discarded on the battlefield?

'Ma Bhawani willing, we will return and reclaim it!' He flung a cheery glance at the others to camouflage his despair.

To his dismay he discovered that the same gloom had settled on their faces too. Bhanmal opened his mouth to say something, then stopped. Perhaps he wanted to tell them about the many battles it had served him in but was afraid of his own effervescing emotions. Jairaj twisted his face into the grimace they were to become familiar with, while Kishan covered his face for a brief moment. When he took his hands away, a ray of the rising sun lit the wetness on his cheeks. And Nathu grunted, as if he were taking on a heavier weight than the one he was discarding.

Lalchand shivered as the early morning wind speared through his quilted *angarkha*. He felt totally exposed now, not only to the elements but to whatever else providence was cooking up for him.

The sounds emerging from the somewhat pitiful cavalcade had seemed distant in the beginning. Cows lowing, an infant crying for its mother's breast, an old man coughing. Only when a woman's prolonged wailing was shaped into words did his head begin to throb. It was a diatribe against fate, against looting invaders, against kings who could not protect their people. Soldiers who could not hold up in the battlefield. An elegy for the familiar life she had been compelled to abandon.

Why? She kept asking, why? Over and over again.

Jogging along listlessly, Lalchand had wondered if he would ever find the answer.

Now, with his hopeful feet bearing him towards yet another unknown destination he realised he was no closer to it.

The Stuff of Dreams

'**Why** do you think we have dreams? Do they mean anything, as people say?' asked the young woman, whose name was Ketaki.

'Dreams are given to us to save our lives,' the old woman replied. She seemed lost in a dream herself when she said this.

'But what if a dream remains incomplete? Or if it's a bad dream? How can a nightmare save our lives?' asked the young woman scornfully. She studied the old woman's face with an impatient frown. 'I'm talking about real dreams, the type you have when you're asleep.'

The old woman's face was scored and criss-crossed with so many lines that one could get lost tracing their course. Trying to find where one ended and the other began would be like trying to find a way out of the maze of time itself. Ketaki had tried often enough but been compelled to give up each time.

'No dream is ever false,' said the old woman after a long time. 'The dreamer may be false to the dream but not the dream to the dreamer. Because ... the dream is you, the essential, inner you ...'

Ketaki sat up suddenly, jerking her hair out of the old woman's hands. She was oiling her hair. Ketaki had long and lustrous hair and the old woman got much pleasure out of handling it. As a professional masseuse, her services were not as much in demand anymore as they used to be and as it was she hardly ever got the opportunity to play with such long hair.

'I had a dream last night,' Ketaki said irritably. 'I don't think it was given to me to save my life.' She was disappointed in the old woman. She was simply looking for comfort but the old woman nattered too much, gave too much unsought-for advice. She made such a big deal of her wisdom and experience but came up with so many nonsensical sounding statements that Ketaki was inclined to believe she was growing senile. She certainly was old enough. 'I believe,' she continued, 'it was given to me to frighten me out of my wits, not save my life. That I could do such a mad thing—even in a dream! The thought! As if I was not afraid enough.' She shuddered. 'If only I knew what it meant. You know so many people. Do you know anyone who interprets dreams?'

'Ah, so that's what you want ...' the old woman said. 'Well, a dream may be a portent, it may be a riddle, but are you sure you want to know? It may not be what you want to hear,' she added in a softer voice.

'Of course! Why else do you think I'm asking you?' Ketaki said, ignoring the last sentence.

'Sometimes it's better not to know too much,' the old woman went on, her voice dry. 'But tell me your dream.'

She massaged Ketaki's head in a smooth, circular motion. The young woman felt a languorous peace steal over her. The old woman might talk too much but she was good at her work. Ketaki's head hurt. She'd been up half the night attending to her husband's needs, which were many—they left her with very little time to sleep, to recoup from the stressful events of the day.

She'd massaged his legs. Then she had suckled him at her breast like a babe. When she was done with that he wanted to crawl into the dark soft place she had which made him forget all his troubles. Sometimes it seemed that he wanted to stay there forever. But he was her husband so she had to do all this for him. She wasn't sure if the headache was the result of too little sleep or the unfinished dream. An unfinished dream leaves you with a sense of frustration, a feeling of incompleteness, a yearning almost as unbearable as unfinished loving.

'Tell me the dream,' the old woman said. 'I know a little about dreams and what they mean.'

'I dreamt that I was walking in the marketplace and a madwoman came up to me. Her hair was knotted and wild, her face caked with dirt, flies buzzed about her in swarms. She wore a dirty old blanket wrapped around her, a thick grey blanket,' Ketaki spoke rapidly as if she wanted to finish telling it as fast as she could. 'But when I looked into her red-rimmed eyes which were so large and untamed, I froze. Something in her eyes held me—as if it was something I could recognise, identify with. Strange, isn't it—what would I have in common with a madwoman from the streets?'

She seemed to address the question to herself but the old woman, the garrulous old woman had to answer. 'Yes,' she said, sounding more like an echo than a person answering a question. 'What would you have in common with a madwoman of the streets?' Her voice was blank, as empty and expressionless as an echo.

'And as I stood there watching her she made a sudden movement and the blanket fell open.' Ketaki paused, as if to reconsider what she was saying. Her voice quivered as she finally said, 'With a shock I realised that she wore nothing underneath that blanket—nothing at all!'

'Nothing at all,' repeated the old woman. Oddly enough she didn't sound at all surprised. She knew more about the ways of madwomen than the young woman who had always lived immured within the safe walls of her house. The old woman's work took here and there, through the busy streets, in and out of houses. She knew practically all there was to know from the business of the streets to the secrets in the big, safe houses—which swarmed as thickly with secrets as the sewers with cockroaches. Secrets which belied their promise of safety.

The young woman sucked in her breath. 'I don't know what I felt at that moment,' she said, 'looking at her nakedness, thinking of her roaming the streets with nothing more than a blanket between her and the world. But whatever I felt at that moment was very strong—so I reached out and took hold of her hand and led her home. I thought I'd give her some clothes to wear, you see ... clothes which would give her some kind of protection. A woman without clothes is so exposed!'

'How kind, what a kind little woman,' murmured the old one. She rubbed Ketaki's head hard, so hard that it shook. But the young woman didn't seem to notice and went on, narrating the story of her dream.

'Well, I took her straight into the bathroom, and pulled off her dirty old blanket and flung it out of the window. I can't tell you how good I felt when I threw the filthy thing away. At that moment I could imagine what the madwoman would feel like when she was nice and clean, dressed in fresh, new clothes—if a madwoman can understand what that feels like! But it would have made me feel much better to see her decently dressed. The thought of another woman so exposed is scary. What had really upset me was the fact that she didn't seem to mind at all, roaming the streets like that all naked under the blanket. She didn't say anything at all when I took her by the hand and led her home. She just clutched my hand as tightly as she could and came along, as trusting as a child. In fact, I had to pry her fingers off when I put her under the shower ... I hope you understand what I'm saying,' she said turning around to look into the old woman's face. 'In this dream I took this dirty, filthy madwoman into my own beautiful bathroom with its gold and white tiles and stood her under my own shower!'

'I understand,' the old woman nodded. 'I understand very well.' There was a touch of asperity in her voice. 'I also understand that it was a dream.'

'Of course it was a dream! Didn't I tell you right in the beginning? But I can't tell you how vivid this dream is still in my mind. It feels as if it really happened.' She shivered a little. 'Now—', the young woman paused, she ran her pointed red tongue over her lips as if they felt dry suddenly. 'She didn't seem to know what to do, you understand? She was that mad. She didn't even know that she had to wash herself. So *I* had to do it for her. I had to pick up the soap and rub it over her body, scrub her clean. I felt a little odd, but I had to do it. I had committed myself to making her clean and fresh again. But …' The young woman paused again, 'My clothes got wet, so I took them off. I thought, what the hell, we were just two women together and she was mad in any case.'

'What logic—such logic in a dream,' the old woman murmured.

'Why can't there be logic in dreams?' the young woman demanded, a little miffed. 'I'm a logical person, you know, and also a kind person, even though I say so myself. Who would want to handle a dirty, mad woman? It's risky, you know, handling a mad person. Who knows when they might turn around and attack you? I'm brave too, you know,' she added, as if just discovering that about herself. 'And in any case—don't I take off my clothes for you to massage me?'

'Yes you do, yes you do,' the old woman's head seemed to wag on its own. 'And yes, my dear, you are kind and brave, very kind and brave.' She stroked the young woman's soft cheek gently. Her hand felt rather rough and scratchy for a masseuse. 'But I hope you're not forgetting that it was a dream.'

'Certainly not!' The young woman sounded injured. 'Do you think I would do such things in real life?'

'No you wouldn't,' the old woman sounded sad. 'I doubt it, very much.'

'By the way—' the young woman said softly, 'she had a beautiful body. Can you imagine,' she said wonderingly, 'a madwoman with a beautiful body? Such high, full breasts, such a slim waist …'

'Why not?' replied the old woman softly. So softly that the young woman did not hear what she said after that. 'Why can't or why shouldn't a madwoman have a beautiful body?' A little louder, she said, 'Take off your blouse my dear, so I can massage your back now.'

The young woman complied, dutifully. She had a beautiful body too, even though she was not mad. 'Ah-h ...' she said, as the old woman rubbed her back. 'That feels so-o good!' The old woman's hands felt softer now ... going up and down, up and down her back ... soothing all the pain away.

'Well—' the young woman continued, 'After I had finished soaping her—mind you—it was like bathing a small child who is unable to bathe herself.' She giggled a little hysterically. 'A small child with breasts and-and pubic hair.' Then she stopped laughing and became a little serious. Actually more than a little serious. She looked quite grim as a matter of fact. 'While I was trying to bathe her I couldn't help noticing that there was blood congealed between her legs ... She'd been—had—'

'We've all been had!' the old woman cried out, so shrill and sudden that the young woman started and let out a little shriek herself. 'And we all bleed when we're had, outwardly or inwardly. I've been had so many times that I've lost count! And I've bled so much—'

'Oh shut up, who wants to keep count of all that,' the young woman replied brusquely. 'I certainly don't. I'd rather forget such things. And if I can return to my dream, please—we're not talking about your bleeding but the madwoman's.'

'Of course, you can,' the old woman sounded annoyed. Maybe there was something more she wanted to say but the young woman was not letting her. And that can be as frustrating for a garrulous old woman as an unfinished dream or incomplete loving for a young one—because after all, ultimately what else is left but words?

'I felt more than a little sick, you know, seeing that. But I had to finish the job. I'd begun to clean her up and I would complete my job as best I could, especially since the poor thing was no more competent than a child. She whimpered and squirmed a little at first, then she seemed to like it—being cleaned up, you know. Then suddenly she began to think that she should do the same thing to me—imagine!' The young woman's laugh rang out, sharp and clear. 'Wasn't it weird? The poor child ...'

'Weird indeed,' said the old woman a little absent-mindedly, as if she were preoccupied with all she couldn't say, all that was going round and round in her mind, the undigested thoughts she couldn't spew out as words, tumbling about here and there inside her head. 'You get yourself massaged every day,' she suddenly said, 'and your body will remain young and alive forever.'

'Too bad you couldn't do the same for yourself,' the young woman said unkindly. She was furious that the old woman insisted on interpolating her stray thoughts into her narrative, disturbing the flow. She also sensed an ulterior motive, a pecuniary one, and she didn't like being reminded of the fact that one day *she* might be like the old woman—criss-crossed with wrinkles.

'Who knows what I could or couldn't do for myself?' the old woman replied indifferently. 'But you haven't told me the rest of your dream.'

'What is there to tell? Just another senseless dream.' The young woman sounded quite irritable. Then she softened. She did want to tell someone and the old woman was the only one she could talk to. 'Well, I told you what she was doing to me,' she giggled. 'And then what do you think happened?'

'What?'

'My husband came home and caught us.'

'What!'

'I'd forgotten to bolt the door, imagine. Wasn't it silly of me? He was angry, so angry, I can't tell you—'

'He was? In your dream?'

'Then—' Ketaki went on as if she hadn't heard. 'After I'd flung on some clothes and told him the whole story—how I'd felt sorry for the madwoman and brought her home to clean her up—he understood. I think he understood. At least I hope so. But he said I couldn't keep her. You know ... I'd thought I could keep her, felt it was my duty to keep her, she wasn't safe on the streets ... she needed someone to take care of her ... being so mad and helpless. I thought she could be the child I haven't had so far ... the sister I've never had or the friend who went away. I would bathe her every day, we'd play together ... but he said no. He said, after you've dressed her and fed her, you send her back to where she came from ... she's dangerous, he said ... madwomen are dangerous ... You can't keep a madwoman in my house, in our house. I felt so sad.' She let out a long weary sigh. 'He also told me not to venture out into the streets again, it was not safe there, with madwomen roaming all over.'

Oddly, the old woman didn't comment on that, she only said, 'I'll massage your legs now.'

'I dressed her up. It was like dressing a child ... or a doll. I dressed her in some of my best clothes. He didn't object, he was so anxious to get rid of her. I think—I think he was scared. She laughed loudly, laughed like a madwoman when I put her in those clothes, stroked my silk sari, put it against her cheek. Then I gave her some food. She didn't know how to eat, I had to feed her with a spoon like you feed a baby. Can you imagine anyone so helpless? And then—I led her out of the door and into the street—I led her by the hand like a child and left her on the street—my dream madwoman. And when she stood there looking at me with her big, wild eyes—I wanted to cry ...'

'You wanted to cry ...'

'But I didn't cry,' the young woman's eyes were big and wild now. 'I didn't want him to see me cry. I crept inside ... but I wanted to look at her once again before she disappeared ... so I peeped out of the window. And what do you think I saw?'

'What did you see?'

'I saw her tearing off the clothes I'd dressed her in. She tore up my lovely silk sari, the matching blouse and petticoat and she tore off the lovely bras and panties I'd put on her, the ones my husband bought on his last trip abroad. And then she picked up the old blanket from the side of the road where I'd thrown it, and put it around her and went away. She didn't turn around to look at me even once ... not even once. I was about to run out of the house after her but then ... I woke up ...'

Then she turned around to look into the old woman's eyes. 'Do *you* think this dream was sent to me to save my life?' Her voice was mocking.

'Maybe, maybe, there is much we cannot understand,' the old woman looked confused now—as if she'd thought that she knew everything but wasn't so sure now. 'But ... perhaps it'll take you some time to find out.'

A loud shriek startled her. It was the young woman, Ketaki. She was tearing off—no, she was trying to tear up her clothes. She had already taken them off for the massage.

'Hush,' said the old woman. 'Hush ...' She held the young woman's arms tightly till she stopped struggling, gave up exhausted. Then she cradled her in her arms. The young woman buried her head in her lap and moaned and whimpered, 'I lied to you, I lied to you ... It was not an incomplete dream ... I didn't tell you the end ... because there was an end ... I ran after her and when she turned around, I saw that her face had changed ... She looked just like me ... no, she had become me—or I had become her!'

The old woman's hands were very soft now—as soft as the silken sari. 'It doesn't matter,' she said, 'it doesn't matter. It was just a dream ...' In a lower voice she said, 'But remember what your husband said ... never venture outside these safe walls. You might bring a madwoman from the streets into your house ... and find yourself!'

Karma

When Radha entered Parmanand Joshi's home as his second wife she was no spring chicken. Sympathisers did cluck and whisper over the fate of this hapless, callow girl. But it wasn't that way.

Nobody had been misled. Parmanand Joshi had made it quite clear that he was marrying Radha so there was someone to nurse his wife—her older sister Durga, who was dying—and to take care of her nephews and niece. The poor children needed their running noses wiped, their tangled locks combed, their battling limbs separated—and who could do it better than their aunt, Radha?

Radha's father had not lied to her mother either. 'It's not the best of matches, nor the worst,' he had said, coughing over his hookah while seated on the threshold of their kitchen, staring over his wife's demurely draped head.

Radha's mother continued to stir the lentils with stoic concentration, as if the heavy brass ladle was consuming all her strength. She had never been one to squander words and in consequence, enjoyed a reputation for sagacity. Her advice was often sought and she gave it in brief, oracular sentences, which left the seeker confused but grateful. After all, an oracle has to be interpreted.

But right now, as she fixes her eyes on the little yellow bubbles exploding on the surface of the battered brass pot her thoughts erupt in an exceptionally lucid statement: 'Radha will earn great merit.' Her husband's gaze swivels from the mud-plastered kitchen walls to rest admiringly on her face.

'You are right.' His rheumy eyes light up. 'Our youngest is far more blessed than her four older sisters. What good karma!'

The blessed girl is crossing the courtyard with a platter of uncooked rice in her hand. The winter sun has flung a cloak of languor around her shoulders. Completely unaware that she's about to add a gleaming patch on that tattered garment—her mother's heart—Radha slouches towards her fate, a secret smile making her red lips twitch.

Her father coughs again and rises. 'I'll be back in a while,' he mumbles.

'Ah, the rice ... Sit down for a moment, child.' Her mother's voice is furry with warmth.

Radha places a cautious step over the threshold. The grime of daily use is slowly obliterating the festive orange and white patterns decorating its ancient wood, but still she tries to protect them.

Her mother pulls out a low wooden stool. Radha's confusion escalates, mottling her face with dark patches. Such consideration—why?

She sinks down on the stool, her plumpish frame displaying a fluid grace, saying, 'I've already washed the rice.'

'Yes, yes, I can see that.' Her mother pushes a few recalcitrant grey wisps of hair into their proper place behind her ear, then lets a deep breath escape. 'Your sister's not getting any better, I'm afraid.'

Radha's tongue immediately bloats, occupying all the space in her mouth.

'Those poor children. Panditji is talking of taking another wife.'

One of the sticks feeding the fire crackles. Sparks shoot out. Radha pushes her stool back hurriedly. But her mother continues as if nothing had happened. 'Child, your father has spoken to him. He is willing to marry you.'

A choked sound escapes Radha, astonishingly like a suppressed giggle. Her mother stops breathing for a moment. But then Radha simply allows her chin to sink into the comfortable cushion of her chest, picks up one end of her faded cotton sari and chews on it.

'Durga will die happy and in comfort now, child.' Her mother sighs, her words as jagged as a lightning flash. The ensuing embrace is awkward. Radha cannot help thinking—is it possible for a thirty-seven-year-old woman with four children to die happily and comfortably?

Her mother does not say anything about the good karma Radha will earn. She doesn't need to. Radha knows.

Radha, the far-from-spring chicken, is twenty-four and a lot like her mother in some ways. Sometimes it even seems as though, along with other essential nutrients, she has imbibed stoicism from her mother's milk. There is one big difference, though. She has been heard giggling frequently, unlike her mother, who hardly ever smiles. These giggles effervesce at the most unlikely of moments—like when she's picking out stones from the rice, or even while the milkman's son Madan is measuring milk into the pot. Her broad shoulders shudder, her large breasts jiggle under her sari, her face acquires a frightening red tinge and her night-black eyes disappear into her round cheeks.

This could also be a reason why her father grabbed this opportunity to marry her off, even if it's to a greyhead. Who knows? What everyone does know is that it's almost impossible to find a suitable match for a Brahmin girl of her age, equal in caste, and with some kind of income. And Parmanand Joshi even owns property.

Everyone also knows that marriage means compromise. How else would the institution survive? Perhaps this aphorism floats in the hazy air of her mother's kitchen, which Radha has been inhaling almost since the day she was born. No doubt the rafters, with their coating of glossy, venerable soot, whisper it to her as she pummels the dough to the appropriate softness.

Radha may have a tendency to giggle but at heart she is a serious girl. She knows that Baujyu's old and it is his duty to get her married before he dies. She knows that it's all right to enjoy an occasional laugh with Madan the milk boy. He is such an amusing fellow, has such a droll turn of speech, such radiantly transparent brown eyes—eyes that stick to hers like honey. It takes all the effort she can muster to wrench hers away. And as for the warmth that trickles through her body—drop by insistent drop—it's impossible to wring it out for a long, long time. But he is a milkman's son.

It's not unheard of to be a second wife, and yes, she will certainly ease her sister's pain. The pain of Durga didi, who has always been so generous about letting her wear her saris and try on her jewellery. And Parmanand Joshi may be almost as grey as her father but he owns two houses, one of which is rented out. This is in addition to the salary he earns as a teacher in the government school. Compared to them, he's positively rich. She doesn't mind marrying him at all. What could be better?

But sometimes, early in the morning, as she hefts the copper water pot onto her hip and sets out to fill it from the spring by the roadside, she cannot help but pause to look up the melting sky. Dense night dissolving into incandescent day. There is a world beyond this, she has heard. Beyond this routine of fetching water, scouring utensils with ash and rolling chapattis.

Once she accompanied her mother to a wedding in another town. They boarded the bus and reached their destination, Ranikhet, retching all the way from the motion of the bus as it swung along the curving road. They arrived, dazed and apprehensive, shakily hoisted down their small tin trunk, slung their cloth bags over their shoulders and located Govind, who had been sent to receive them, with relieved smiles. Her mother's sister was richer than them. Sometimes Radha felt that everyone was richer than them. She tried to restrain such thoughts. It seemed disloyal to her father.

They had entered a courtyard so crowded with bright new copper pots and shiny brass platters that her eyes widened in disbelief. Her cousin Gauri's dowry was displayed in two rooms, for all to take note of—saris tied up with auspicious red and yellow *kalava* thread, the tablecloths Gauri had been embroidering for years, bedspreads, gold jewellery, furniture so slick with polish that your fingers slid off it. And of course the marital bed, with its auspicious red cover.

The guerrilla sting of the nettles that sometimes reached out from the hillsides to pinch her, tingled unexpectedly on Radha's arms.

She threw a sly, speculative glance at Gauri, crouched on the floor, dressed in an old sari, her hair dishevelled, waiting for turmeric paste to be rubbed on the slender bamboo frame of her body, to lighten her already pale skin, make her glow for her bridegroom. She looked as if she didn't know whether to be happy or frightened.

An old woman staggered in, leaning on a stick, and glowered at her aunt. 'This is all very well, Leela, but I hear you're sending this child to the plains—to die in the heat.'

A thin, rueful smile spread over her aunt's face and an appealing glance slid towards Radha's mother's expressionless face. But it failed to elicit any kind of support. Finally Radha's aunt was forced to reply, tugging nervously at her necklace. 'The family's very good, kaki. Absolutely the right caste. Best, the boy has a government job.'

'Government-phovernment! And what if she falls sick in the heat? Don't we all know how delicate our Gauri is?'

This time Radha's mother spoke up, saying, 'It's her fate, kaki, which will decide. Whatever the one above has willed for her.'

The murmur of approval clogged Radha's ears. Her aunt looked grateful. The cantankerous relative grunted scornfully and knocked one of the trousseau saris, a brilliant pink silk, off the bed as she stumped her way out.

Radha's eyes stick to Gauri. They are the same age but hardly know each other. That distance of fifty-six kilometres has been too great to bridge. Gauri has translucent skin, through which you can see fine blue veins tracing a feathery path up her arms. Her eyes are translucent too, a greenish-brown, her pink lips are sharply curved.

Radha sinks to the floor next to her. 'You lucky girl,' she whispers, squeezing her hand. The tiny bones feel frighteningly brittle. 'You'll get to travel in a train. Does one get sick in a train too, like in a bus?'

Gauri smiles gratefully and Radha feels that despite their poverty, she and her mother have something which Gauri and her aunt don't. 'No,' she says. 'We went to Bareilly last winter, you don't get sick. You can even stretch out your legs and sleep on the berth.' The idea of stretching out her legs and sleeping in a train takes hold of Radha so powerfully that her stomach aches.

She will travel in a train one day, when she's much older, when the wonder of such journeys has been somewhat flattened by the weight of time. She will journey to live with her nephew and stepson, Taraknath, in Lucknow and experience the heat of the plains herself. She'll stretch out her legs on a narrow, wooden berth, sandwiched between a snoring man and a young girl who sleeps sweetly on her stomach.

But Gauri will not attend Radha's wedding. She will be pregnant with her second child and Radha will be relieved. Her brother-in-law doesn't look any better as a bridegroom. The red and white dots painted around his eyebrows look misplaced, as does the tinsel crown. His face looks too weary to sport such finery to any effect.

She has been emptying herself out, a little at a time, since the date was finalised. But when she throws a covert glance at him from under her eyelashes, seated beside him before the fire which is witnessing the irrevocability of their union, she realises she has not emptied herself enough. There is still something left, enough to make her feel as if she is riding that bus to Ranikhet, which churned her insides out.

But later, changing into the maroon velvet ghaghra he has brought for her, dressed in which she will enter his house—a resplendent bride—she feels like a wisp of air, inconsequential, almost non-existent. She does not really experience the journey from one end of town to the other in the swaying palanquin. But an odd feeling of joy illuminates her when she sees Didi standing at the door to welcome her with lighted lamps. She experiences fear too, at the sight of her wan face, which contrasts too starkly with the brightness of her festive attire.

And in an inexplicable way, life acquires a sameness to what it was before. Getting up in the morning, fetching water, lighting the fire, putting the kettle to boil for tea, then making dal, rice, whatever vegetables are to be cooked. There is no giggling with Madan the milk boy though—there is a cow to milk instead.

Didi, who has taken to her bed again, keeps handing out instructions: 'Panditji likes his tea with black pepper in it ... Put plenty of red chillies in the spinach … The dal didn't have enough ghee yesterday …'

A coughing fit will invariably interrupt her after which she'll fall back on her bed. The ensuing silence settles on Radha like frost, she feels tiny grains of it line her skin, stiffen it the way blades of grass congeal in the backyard in winter. Waiting helplessly for the hesitant tendrils of sunlight to coil around them, to perform their magic and set them free.

People had told her, 'You're lucky. You won't have a mother-in-law to harass you. And even if you're a step-mother, aren't they your own sister's children?'

On good days Durga didi totters to the kitchen and tries to cook a dish the way Panditji likes it. Radha watches silently, ignores the coughing. She knows she should drag Didi away, make her lie down but she dare not. This is Didi's kitchen, her house, her husband, her children.

When Panditji summons her to his room at night she knows she is a stand in for Didi, or rather an impersonator, like the ghost who took the form of the prince in the story and slept with the princess. She wonders if Didi can hear the creaking of the bed and Panditji's grunts of pleasure.

When she creeps back to her bed in the children's room, Didi's cough pursues her. One day she calls out, 'Radha …' in a voice so low and yet so penetrating that she has to flee to her bed and lie there, as still as a rock, hating herself. Is she sick, should she attend to her? But a wintry frost imprisons her body, she cannot move.

The next time Didi calls out, however, her voice as brittle as the paper in one of Panditji's old books, she is compelled to stop, straighten her crumpled sari and tip-toe to her room. She forces herself to embrace the reek of sickness, like a cleansing punishment.

'What is it, Didi,' she asks. 'Can I get you some water?' She places a kettle in the embers all night so that there is warm water for Didi to drink.

'No,' Didi replies. Her eyes are painfully bright in the liquid dark. Radha stands there, wondering what to offer next. Does her head ache? Does she need to be escorted to the lavatory outside?

'You have sharp ears,' Didi says grudgingly. 'No ... yesterday you didn't hear me. Perhaps you were sound asleep. I just wanted to tell you that I know you will nurse me back to health. I know I'll be all right.' Her voice chokes on the intensity of her hope. 'I'll soon be able to attend to Panditji's needs.'

It takes Radha a while to speak. She marvels that her voice can flow out so smoothly; it doesn't seem to belong to her. 'Of course you will, Didi.' She touches her hot dry hands. 'Of course.'

You will get all right and I'll fly away into the night like the ghost I am, search for the milk boy in his village. The wind knocking on the windowpanes will carry me on its back. But a silent, acid laughter stirs inside her. She has to hurry away before it boils over.

The next day when Panditji summons her, she pleads exhaustion. She knows, however, that the excuses will soon dry up. And the following night, when he dances a gold necklace before her, she cries, 'That's Didi's!'

'So it is,' he says. 'What's the difference? What's hers is yours too—like me.' The smile doesn't sit well on his face.

She says, 'You married me to nurse her and take care of the children. I'm doing that well enough. If you expect anything more, I'll run away.'

'You'll leave your sister to suffer and die alone?'

'She would have done that in any case.' Where does this hardness come from, Radha wonders, as she watches Panditji's incredulous face.

She walks away as silently as she can, dreading the coughs that might halt and the whisper that might rustle through the night, 'Radha ...'

But Didi does not call out.

The nights stretch themselves out, if not smoothly, at least uneventfully.

In the end, Didi's hope is not strong enough, nor is Radha's nursing effective enough.

But Radha lives to see Taraknath put the torch to his father's pyre. She assumes the widow's white, and her mother's enigmatic expression stamps itself on her face so clearly that she finds the role of oracle has been handed to her—an unwanted, unasked for legacy. People have always wondered why she didn't have any children. Some say it's for the best. Others say it's not good. Panditji always remained silent when such questions were asked.

Radha spent a few nervous nights after Didi's death but the summons never came. Maybe he understood, maybe he was afraid, maybe he no longer had needs. Who knows what's going on inside a man's head? Radha was relieved.

But sometimes when she's hanging up the clothes to dry, she pauses to gaze at the sky stretching above the fecund green of the terraced fields, which coil away from her, above the massed mystery of the deodar trees. The wind carries the heat of the milk boy's breath to her cheeks, the fleeting touch of his hand on hers as he pours a stream of white liquid into the vessel she holds out. The milk foams as he measures it. They are too poor to afford much and the milk fills the pot only halfway. But sometimes, smiling from beneath his eyelashes like a conspirator, he would add half a measure more so it almost reached up to the brim.

Maybe in my next birth, she thinks, it will be different.

The Crossing

The stars still shone out of the navy-blue sky when Sandip woke them. Anuradha was awake at once, sensing rather than hearing his call. There was an impulse, electric, urgent, which made her spring out of bed—even though she wasn't fully awake.

'Yes,' she muttered, foggily aware of the shape at the window. 'I'm awake.' Her heart beat unevenly—trying to adjust its rhythm from slumber to sudden wakefulness.

The stars looked bitingly cold, embedded in the dull, cellophane translucence. But she lingered at the window even after Sandip drifted away, seeking out the hill they were going to climb. With its sharp, twisty peak, it was usually quite distinct from the other, more gently-moulded hilltops. Right now, though, it looked vague, indefinite, almost a part of the sky.

That's where I'm going, she thought, feeling her belly tingling.

'Do you want to use the loo first?' Coming out of the dark, Poonam's sleep-thickened voice startled her. It sounded oracular, anonymous as a stranger's.

'All right,' she said, smiling a little. Poonam hated getting up early, savoured those extra precious minutes in bed. But as she turned, she became painfully aware of a crick in her neck. Irritation spasmed. Of all the days to wake up with a stiff neck!

Clumsy, she crab-walked to the bathroom and sluiced herself with tepid water. She dressed, tugged a comb through her short coarse hair, her body going through the motions like a correctly programmed robot. But her mind kept veering around to the hill—that unreal, improbable destination. On those smooth, soft evenings when they sat outside, faintly curtained by the darkness, a little befuddled by the chilly, overly-sweet scent of the *raat ki rani*, the lights from that hill had twinkled a secret, alluring message at her. Of a life remote, magical, removed from everything she had ever known and experienced. Of an existence, high, safe and snugly secluded.

So when Sandip had suggested the trek, she'd been the one who'd first cried out, 'Yes, let's go there!' her round, normally placid face aglow. Even though she'd never done that sort of thing before.

But she hadn't done this sort of thing before either—walked away from home. Or rather—not returned. Her very presence here was an act of rebellion, open defiance of her mother's wishes. She'd always been a good daughter, eager to please, obey, and never rock the boat. So much so, that she often forgot what she had done. So removed was this course of action, so alien to her nature, that she forgot that this wasn't just a holiday visit to a friend. But when she remembered, as she did right now, a tiny needle began to bore into her, deeper and deeper, diffusing a horrible, tingling uncertainty. What had she done? Where was she headed?

Perhaps she hadn't expected it to turn out like this. She'd expected her mother to pursue, threaten or coax her back. Mollify her by announcing an immediate cancellation of the marriage arranged for her against her wishes—which had provided the provocation. She had hoped that her mother would realise that she was tired of being led by the nose, that she had wishes, desires of her own too.

But, more likely, deep down she'd known that Amma would not follow any such form of action. It was not like her to coax or wheedle. She ordered and people obeyed—especially Anuradha.

And yet—could anyone react like that? When a daughter whose marriage date has been finalised decides not to return home—could anyone acknowledge the event with a hollow, echoing silence? A silence like a still, dark well that goaded one to throw stones into it, so at least you could see movement, ripples—anything that disturbed that unnerving depth.

And she had achieved it ultimately. There had been a ripple, a tremendous wave, rather. Maybe she had expected that too, was prepared for it. She had invited it, certainly, with that provocative, challenging letter. The second letter she'd written to her mother.

The first, written from the hostel, probably betrayed her uncertainty. Made her mother smile, perhaps, after her first fury had abated. So it was possible that that silence was calculated, designed to unhinge her, bring her to heel.

She had been shaken by that silence but not frightened. Angered rather, by the lack of response, of recognition of the fact that she'd left home. As if that silence negated the reality of her action, made it appear as if it hadn't happened at all. As if she did not exist, had no connection with her mother.

How impatiently she had waited for her reply after she left the hostel and went home with Poonam! She had been apprehensive, of course, knowing her. Suppose Amma decided to come and haul her back bodily? What would she do? When it didn't happen, self-recrimination took over. Had she wounded her mother so much, that she was shattered, laid low? She had spent many days wondering if she might even have fallen ill. But as the arid, response-less days trickled by, silent and inexorable as sand flowing through an hourglass, she had felt confused. A burgeoning knot of pain had replaced the confusion. Was this all it deserved—this momentous decision of hers—and from her own mother? Did she mean so little that she could be totally ignored, her existence erased?

And so she sent that letter which could not, would not be ignored.

'What does it say?' Poonam had asked. She too, had been waiting for the reply, along with Anuradha. Perhaps she had run through the same gamut of emotions, as her thin, taut face revealed when she took the letter from the postman and handed it to Anuradha.

Anuradha had paled.She had not been able to control the little tremor that shook her hand as she opened the letter. She had felt her face flame as she read it, felt it go hotter and hotter, till the blood rang in her ears.

'I've been disowned,' she'd said gaily, through frozen lips, letting it slip from her hands. Her first impulse had been to crumple it, fling it as far as she could. But she had resisted it. Like her mother, she'd decided to minimise her response, swallow the pain in one swift gulp. Poonam's face had stiffened, then creased into lines of sympathy. 'Don't worry,' she'd said, her slender frame bending forward comfortingly.

Anuradha had shrugged again, though a huge black space was opening up inside, expanding so fast that she was afraid that she'd disintegrate any minute.

And if Pratap and Nikki (Poonam's cousins) hadn't appeared just then and suggested a walk down to town, who knows what might have happened. Even now, though it had been a whole week since she received the letter, an awful chill numbed her whenever she remembered. In the midst of conversation, she would freeze, conscious that things were different now, that she had been abandoned. There was no solid supportive presence behind her. She was all on her own, stumbling off into the dark to some unknown place.

Sometimes an insidious fear slithered over her in the middle of the night, crawling out of her dreams. She'd wake up with a start, shaken by uncontrollable rigors, which would leave her feeling as raw and vulnerable as an open wound. And she would lie awake, thinking and thinking, till the darkness dissolved and the hard pale light stung her eyeballs. In a sense, her second letter had been an attempt to reaffirm her connection with her mother. So she had been totally unprepared for that relentless slashing of bonds.

But these moments were becoming rarer. If her mother could be unrelenting, so could she. Because—and at times she could hate herself for it—there was also an exhilaration, an evanescent fluttering. As though she could take off from one of these hills and fly to another at will. Float. Fall free like the wheeling birds that rode the currents all day. Take off confidently, knowing the air (however unsubstantial it might appear) would hold her up.

The trek had become even more important to her since she received the letter. She could not understand why. But she felt an almost uncontrollable restlessness—urging her on, away from this scene, this place where pain still hung around her, its scent fresh and raw, to the challenge of something new.

'Ready, Anu?' Poonam's voice was nasal, obstructed—as though she had a cold.'I'm getting the food.'

'All right.' Hurriedly, Anuradha pulled the covers over the bed, tightened her shoelaces, picked up her knapsack and walked out.

Sandip, Nikki and Pratap waited outside, looming hazily through the darkness.

'Shall we start?' Without waiting for an answer, Sandip began to trudge up the dirt track that led away from the house—towards the town, and ultimately the hill.

They followed.

It felt strange, padding off in the wispy darkness. Her knapsack tugged painfully at her neck. But perversely, she nursed that discomfort, and would not adjust it to ease the ache. She felt nothing right now. None of the urgency, the need for haste that made Sandip stride so briskly. There was no sense of adventure, no excitement. Only the muzzy feeling, the dullness which was the result of waking up at 4:30 in the morning. A kind of disorientation at being on the move when she should have been snug in bed. She felt distant, removed from the others. They seemed alien, like strangers, as they trudged along, insulated from each other by the greyness.

Vaguely she took note of Sandip's stocky figure higher up on the slope. He halted briefly, turned to check if they were following, then went on. He had insisted that they leave early so they could complete most of the climb before the sun grew too strong. He was the only experienced trekker among them. Neither Nikki, small, skinny but with a wiry resilience, nor Pratap, exuberant, articulate, but oddly silent right now, had trekked that far before. Nor had Poonam. And she, of course, was a complete novice.

She tried to quicken her step, keep a regular pace, in spite of Poonam, who walked erratically beside her. She seemed so wonderstruck at the thought of setting off at this hour that she had to pause now and again and look around her, as if to make sure they were actually on their way.

The house was dimly visible. It appeared somnolent, still with the night, and in a different time-zone altogether, because for them the day had already begun.

If I had gone back, Anuradha thought, I would be almost married by now. Almost. She tried to imagine herself in the throes of trousseau collecting—agonising over unstitched blouses, unmatched sandals, purses, cosmetics, jewellery, household apparatus. She imagined herself as the centre of it all—floating atop that feverish effervescence a wedding seemed to produce.

What had made her balk, refuse what she should have accepted calmly—joyfully, rather—as her inevitable fate?

The man's photograph floated up before her eyes—a bland, inoffensive face. Anonymous, a stranger's face. Strange that she should have a stronger recollection of the photograph, rather than the actual person whom she'd met. The grave, perhaps tense young man who had asked her all the expected questions, in a somewhat mechanical manner—as if they had been learned by rote. To which she had given dull, truthful answers, feeling herself thicken by degrees and turn dense, so dense that she could not respond to the sudden smile that ended the interrogation, which perhaps signalled that a test had been successfully passed.

'No! No!' she had cried out when Amma had smilingly confirmed what she'd suspected. 'I can't live with that—that person!' Because that's what he felt like—someone nameless, unreal—just a person.

Amma's face had chilled her. 'Stop being childish! You have to get married.'

Granted, it had appeared to be the perfect match. But she had sensed desperation in her mother's insistence. As if this might be her last chance. As if she were perishable, like a piece of fruit that might rot if left too long on the branch ...

They were walking through the town now—past shuttered shop fronts, through grubby streets where yesterday's garbage festered on the ground. The stench of decay, hung around them, like the dark—faint and cloudy.

Suddenly, street dogs appeared in a clamorous pack. The sound of their barking drummed painfully through the cottony stillness. Pratap stooped to fling a stone at them. They retreated—some yelped—though none of them had been hit. They continued to bark, from a safer distance. She was hard put to control the desire to run.

It was a relief to descend into a pine forest again after that. They filed after Sandip, who still marched ahead, important, full of purpose. The leader, who knew the way.

'Isn't it wonderful, being out at this time,' Poonam whispered. Her sleep-rumpled face was still ecstatic.

'Yes!' Anuradha began to nod but the crick in her neck stopped her short.

Was it the darkness that made them speak in whispers? As if their voices might disturb someone who still slept—the pines perhaps, who stood around them, wrapped in their private silences. And suddenly she was reminded of her mother again. Would it have been better if she had maintained that silence? Or sent a letter as subdued as a whisper, not one like an outraged yell? At least it would not have led to that break, she thought, feeling the soft pine needles, damp with the morning dew, squishing beneath her feet. But the silence itself implied a break. No, her own action was the break. The silence was merely its consequence—the nothing that remained when bonds were severed.

She had always been aware that a daughter's links were tenuous. And once she left, she could not return. As a guest perhaps, but not with the same freedom, the same sense of belonging. But a daughter who flouted her mother's wishes, what chance did she have to return, even as a guest?

Still, she had felt the need to fill that silence with something. Even if it were her suppurating grievances. Or had she felt the need to explain, justify her actions?

' ... And since I am a burden to you ...' (she had written in that letter, the second one). 'I have decided to remove myself and carry that weight on my own. Thanks to you (and what a double-edged statement that was) I am now capable of doing it. The law recognises my ability to make my own decisions—why can't you? Is it so essential that I tie myself to someone you have picked out, when I don't want it? Are my own wishes so unimportant?' How stilted it sounded—but it was true, so true. She had known she was not being educated for any particular purpose. Only because it was required socially. It also helped to use up that uncomfortable period of time during which a suitable match was being arranged. And it was convenient for her mother that she remain at the hostel, leaving her without the problems a grownup daughter can entail. The constant watching and guarding, keeping her spotless, pure, till she could be passed on to the person to whom she properly belonged. And how neatly everything had fallen into place. Within the last six months that remained for her to complete her MA, the perfect match had been located and approved of. And actually nothing remained after that but to complete the ceremony which would allow Amma to dust her hands off and be free of her maternal duties, particularly pressing in Amma's case since her father wasn't there to share the burden.

But she had spoiled it all. No doubt she was already being reviled as an unnatural, thoughtless daughter. Her mother was receiving the sympathy that was her due as the abandoned parent. Perhaps she had been selfish, thought of herself rather than her mother. But why was it demanded of her—that she offer herself up as the sacrifice?

They were out of the forest now, walking down a broadish, paved road that sloped downwards. An incongruity in that remote forest setting. Who could have cobbled that road and when? It was an ancient piece of work—the stones worn slippery smooth, making descent a tricky business. She could hear the regular, monotonous murmur of flowing water, and she realised that the road sloped down to a river.

The sky had lightened considerably. There was a tea shop close by and Sandip had already stopped there. 'Chai break!' he called out.

Anuradha slipped off her knapsack. Pratap stopped, stretched and yawned, then sat down on the low stone wall that ran along the edge of the road. Poonam fished out the sandwiches they'd brought. They sat there munching, sipping hot tea while the water foamed and tumbled below them.

'The tough part begins now,' Sandip said frowning at the river.

Anuradha looked at the hill. It rose sheer and high, straight up from the river. Shrubs and trees crowded its flanks in an untidy jumble. There was nothing of that matte blueness she'd glimpsed day after day. One of the illusions distance created. What would it be like on top, she wondered?

'Okay, let's start,' Sandip said, putting his glass down with a pronounced `ting'.

'Are we supposed to cross the river—like that?' Poonam asked.

'Yes,' Nikki nodded. His grin held a hint of malice. 'There was a bridge of sorts. I believe it was washed away last year.'

Anuradha stared at the narrow plank of wood spanning the gushing rivulet. She felt a harsh chill settle on her. The excitement, the anticipation ebbed, vanished in one swift moment.

'I don't think I can,' she heard Poonam say, her voice dwindling in her throat, eaten up by her terror.

Suddenly her own fear seemed to vanish, confronted with Poonam's greater distress. 'Of course you can,' her own voice rang out uncomfortably smug. 'It's nothing, nothing at all.'

'No—I can't,' Poonam quavered. 'Isn't there any other way?'

She looked at them again, the rushing river, the narrow plank. Felt a sudden exhilaration.

'No, there isn't,' Sandip said with dispassionate finality.

She saw the hill again, its lights beckoning. Her longing to go forward was so strong ... blotting out the streaky dawn that grew above the river.

'Come on!' she urged Poonam. She rose, walked down to the river like a sleep-walker and stepped on to the plank. She could feel that first over-springy step. The plank swayed and she felt a nauseous sweat chill her brow, sick and clammy.

She stepped on it gingerly, her insides molten, shapeless. Suddenly a sliver of sunlight pierced her eyes—unnervingly bright. She felt her foot slide off the plank ... A moment of pure fear—vivid and sudden as a flash of lightning—engulfed her, dimming the cries from the bank behind her as she came down hard—astride the plank. A numb, paralysing terror gripped her as she gazed into the water boiling beneath. Then came an overpowering urge to succumb, pour herself away into the swift torrent, let it carry her off on its own volition ...

Sandip's voice broke the spell, perhaps. But she had already pulled herself up by the time he had stepped on to the plank to help and edged her way to solid ground.

A flutter still pulsed in her chest, a memory, a faint remnant of her fear as she sat on the bank, shaking her head at Poonam's anxious queries. She'd come across in a trice—anxiety erasing her fear.

And something like the calm she had felt when she was on the train, en route to Poonam's house, came over her as she gazed at the foaming water, distant now, no longer magnetic, mesmerising. Would Amma have cared if she had succumbed to its allure? What a beautiful revenge it could have been! What a perfect escape!

The impulse seemed infantile now, ridiculous as she glanced away, up at the hill that towered above her. She could see the road, steep, rocky, visible for a short distance—then losing itself among the shrubbery, the sharp-scented evergreens.

She thought of the hills behind it, layer upon layer upon layer. If she walked and walked, she could traverse them all, perhaps. And what lay beyond—who knew?

And breathing in the tangy air she thought of Amma—alone, sunk in the well of her exclusion—and knowledge burst upon her. She knew what lay beyond those hills ... She'd find it one day, the way home, and find Amma again. But ... only after she'd traversed all those hills ...

If the Earth Should Move . . .

She had never learned to swim. But she dreamt, often, of floating on a wide expanse of water—formless fluid holding her up—her body moving along with its motion—the sun on her face—dancing on the water—a million restless specks of fragmented light ...

The earth—solid, firm, hard—held you upright and still. You could sit or lie down upon it, inhaling the scent of grass and soil, or roll on it, but the motion would be yours. The earth seldom moves. And when it does, it's a disaster.

And what about the air? The air cannot hold you up. You cannot fly like a bird. But there are times when it presses against you, thick as the earth, stopping your breath. It encases you like a prison wall—the air you breathe, the air that is your life. It moves, of course, but does not carry you along like water—the primeval fluid in which we were all formed and lived ...

Mansi felt the baby move with terrific force, tear its way out of her, forcing an enormous scream from her throat. A cry she could not arrest, even if she tried. It went on and on, like a stone, suddenly dislodged, tumbling down a hill, which cannot stop till it reaches the bottom. Only when there was no more sound left within her to wrench out, did it stop.

Then she became conscious of another sound—the baby's long thin wail. It made her feel strangely light-headed. Another being was entering the world. Suddenly she felt a great weariness, as if she already knew what lay ahead of her and sure enough, the very next minute the doctor spoke. 'You've had another girl,' she said.

The air crushed Mansi down with its weight ...

That night she dreamt that she was swimming. She was swimming in a lake surrounded by tall hills. It was a sunny day. The sky was a transparent blinding blue and ahead of her a man moved along, rowing a boat. He wore a short-sleeved T-shirt and she could see that his arms were thickly muscled. So was his smoothly moving back. The boat cut through the water effortlessly, leaving a frothy wake. She badly wanted to see the man's face. In fact she was following the boat just because she was so eager to see what he looked like ... if the face fulfilled the promise of that body.

The baby was pretty. All her daughters were pretty, luckily or unluckily. For a woman, beauty was both a blessing and a curse. She thought of the matrimonial columns in the newspapers, all repetitions of '... wanted—tall, fair, beautiful girl ...' There was something so vapidly monotonous about it. One day she was sure, some high-tech whiz kid would set up a factory to clone the perfect female to satisfy this hunger for tall, fair, beautiful girls.

Her cousin Nisha could have been the perfect model for one of those cloning factories. Nisha, who had introduced her to the glitzy glamour of stars' lives via film magazines. She hadn't realised at the time that Nisha had had aspirations herself. That she was deeply conscious of her own beauty, of the fact that she was star material. That she felt she only needed a hand up from the right quarter, which had not been forthcoming so far. In the tiny *mofussil* town where they lived, what opportunity was there for a girl to further such ambitions?

Nisha had been staying with them at the time. At eleven, Mansi hadn't really been aware of the fact that there had been a particular reason behind Nisha's frequent visits. She had gotten used to her staying with them more than with her own family.

It was not until she heard Nisha talking to her mother that she got a hint as to what was going on. She had sounded frantic saying, '*Mausi*, please, please don't send me back!'

The urgency in her voice had sent something crawling up Mansi's back, made her stomach crumple into a tiny, painful ball. A horrible sensation that told her with plummeting certainty that things were not quite what they seemed. That something ugly and unknown lay beneath the seemingly natural sequence of Nisha's stays. The playful camaraderie that she shared with her, despite the fact that she was almost eight years her senior, which had been growing into a closer, tighter bond during those unscheduled, unexpected visits, suddenly seemed false and unreal, because Nisha had never told her the truth ...

'But your mother wants you back,' Ma had sounded equally frantic. 'How can I refuse her?'

'I am eighteen now,' that stubborn note had entered Nisha's voice. Mansi knew that note. It meant that nothing could move her now. 'I can do what I want. Get married if I wish to. No one can stop me.'

'Do what you want,' her mother's voice had turned hard. 'But do it at your parents' place.'

'Parents? Parents' place?' Nisha's voice had sounded mocking. She had laughed harshly. A sound like the dry rasp of fallen leaves, suddenly disturbed by an unexpected breeze.

Mansi had felt an unexpected anger burgeon up against her mother. Why was she forcing Nisha didi to go back when she didn't want to?

One thing she could guess at, quite easily, was why Nisha wouldn't want to go back. It was because she had a stepfather. Stepfathers were almost unheard of, in the world in which they lived, it was very unusual having one. But Mansi could well believe that they could be as cruel as the proverbial stepmother.

'Nisha didi,' she had whispered that night as they snuggled together in bed. 'Does he beat you?

'Beat me—who?'

'Your—um ... *Mausa* ...'

'Beat me—no, he wouldn't dare—the creep—' She had let out a long jagged sigh, as piercing as a shard of broken glass. 'I hate him, I hate him, I hate him—' she'd stopped abruptly.

'Doesn't *Mausi* tell him not to be mean to you?'

A short bitter laugh. '*Mausi*! *Mausi* can't tell anybody anything. And—she's not going to tell me either!'

All the same, Nisha had had to go. She had looked grim when she left, her eyes had stared blankly through Mansi when she said goodbye, as if she weren't there at all. Mansi had felt hurt. Wasn't Nisha didi sorry to leave her?

A neighbour had happened to be travelling that way. She'd been put in his charge. After all, a young girl could hardly be permitted to travel alone.

It had turned out to be a disastrous choice. Sometime later the news arrived that the two had eloped. The neighbour had abandoned his wife for Nisha. Ma said she would never be able to hold up her head again. She publicly declared that she had broken off all connection with Nisha. Her name was never mentioned again in the house and Mansi had never dared to ask.

And then, years and years later, by some bizarre twist of fate, she had found her again. Married now, Mansi was living in Bombay, a place as remote, as far removed as it was possible, from the small town in which she had grown up. The mother of two girls herself, she had recognised the plumpish matron with a teenaged daughter in tow when she glimpsed her by chance in a store because Nisha's amazing beauty was still more or less intact. She was respectably married now, to a man much older than her. Mansi had never been able to discover exactly what he did for a living, though. Nisha had been evasive.

Mansi swam and swam but could not catch up with the man. She was not able to see his face.

Saurabh hid his disappointment well. He picked up the baby and stroked her soft cheek, 'She looks like you,' he said. Mansi tried to smile, despite the sense of failure that weighed her down.

Was he the man in the dream, who would not show his face, she wondered? In a sense, it would be like him. He was good at concealing his essential self. In all these years of living together, she hadn't found out what he was really like. But, no, he did not have such a spectacular body. Was she secretly hankering for another man? What was it like sleeping with two different men? Nisha would know …

Ultimately, the neighbour had gone back to his wife. But Ma had never spoken to him again. She held him responsible for 'spoiling' Nisha.

'A married man! We trusted him to look after her like a sister,' Mansi had heard her telling her friend Mrs Sharma. 'Imagine my position. Nisha's mother stopped talking to me—my one and only sister. That just shows no man can be trusted.'

But was Nisha totally blameless? Mansi had wondered. Of course, you could blame it on her pretty face. But even Mansi had noticed the coy glances she threw at Ravi bhaiya, another neighbour's son. But would she have deliberately thrown herself at a married man? That was what had always troubled Mansi.

Of course, later, much later when certain facts had become clear to her, she had not been surprised at her desperation.

'We were sleeping outside. It was summer. I felt someone fumbling at the string of my salwar. I was about to scream, when he pressed my mouth shut. I thrashed about hard enough to almost topple the bed over. But you know Ma … she sleeps like a log …'

Perhaps Nisha had thought the neighbour a better option if she had to put up with someone …

'She's a darling, really sweet, mmmm,' Nisha kissed the baby noisily. For some reason Saurabh didn't really like her visiting Mansi, but could hardly stop her. 'She'll grow up to be a beauty, a star.'

Mansi had not been able to hold back a sigh. 'Why are you sighing?' Nisha had demanded. 'Thank God for this lovely baby.'

Lovely baby, lovely baby. Sometimes she was the swimmer and sometimes the lake. The baby swam out of her thrashing wildly. The man in the boat paddled on and on …

'Do you know I went to see him when he was sick, dying?' Nisha said. 'I-I did get in touch with Ma after some time … a long, long time, actually … after all … she was my mother.' There was a strange, inscrutable look on her face. 'Ma insisted that I come. She said he was very eager to see me. He caught hold of my hand. I almost threw up. "Forgive me" he said. Ma told me "He cared for you like his own daughter and you stabbed him in the back like that. We would have got you married in the best way possible. Found you a proper man. You cut off all our noses. We had no face left to show anyone." I didn't know whether to laugh or to cry. Only ... only Sonu, my brother understood. "I know why you went, Nisha didi," he said. He wept. "If I'd been a little older ... but I was too scared of him." Did you know he used to "discipline" Sonu?' Nisha went on. 'Everyone used to praise him ... said he was saint, taking on a widow with two children and not having any of his own. All bullshit. There was something wrong with him. He couldn't have any, I think ... That's why he felt so safe ... with me ...'

Sometimes, when Saurabh lay next to her, holding her close, she felt a smooth syrupy contentment steal over her. The same sensation she had when she swam through her dreams. The sun seeping through her limbs, floating along with the diamond-studded current, further and further ...

But that night, the unexpected happened. She felt herself tiring as she swam. She heard someone crying ... was it herself? Or was it the baby? She could feel it burrowing into her breast. The soft little rosebud mouth turned surprisingly hard when it latched on to her nipples. It tugged and tugged, frantic to get as much as it could out of her ...

No, life is not a straightforward motion, a river flowing onwards. It's a zigzagging movement back and forth—leaving the past to embrace the future, but coming face to face with it again just when you begin to believe you've rounded the bend.

Nisha had made a clean start but yet, the past hung around her like an odour, a whiff of something stale which keeps surfacing no matter how much you try to scrub it away.

'I sometimes wonder why I went off with Naresh. But at the time he seemed like the only option left to me. It was him or back to that ... he swore he was crazy about me. I believed him. *Mausi* must have been furious.'

Her large, questioning eyes were shadowed with an ancient pain.

Mansi nodded expressionlessly, not meeting her gaze. She felt an unexpected guilt stab her, as though she had been a part of that anger, that ostracization. She reached out to stroke the baby's arm, feeling its soft little hand closing tightly around her finger. How strong that instinct was ... to hold on, to clutch for support. Had Nisha felt like that at the time ...? Had she clung on to Naresh like a drowning man clutches at the proverbial straw?

'He said he'd take me to Bombay. He had an uncle in the film line. He would help me, he said, give me a break. He said, "You're more beautiful than any film star ..."' Nisha's eyes seemed to float off, far away, as if she were re-entering that distant time. The moment swung between them, like an indolent pendulum, then slowly carried them back to the present. Nisha shook her head hard, blinked, sniffed surreptitiously. Mansi could feel her heart, a cold lump of iron pressing against her chest ... 'We came here, to Bombay ...' her voice sounded hollow and distant, as if it were coming out of the past ... 'But the uncle had moved. We could not find his new address ...'

Nisha stopped there. As if those things that remained were best left unsaid, even now, at a time so far removed that they almost seemed unreal. Mansi tried to imagine what had happened, how they had coped. And what had ultimately made

Naresh abandon Nisha to return to his young wife and child and of course, his parents. He had a safe niche waiting for him in his father's business. And then, everything is forgiven in the case of the prodigal son … he is always welcomed back.

But the prodigal daughter … Can she find her way home? No. For her coming back is much more complicated. In any case, Nisha, the perennial wanderer, had never had a home in that sense. So she had stayed back, battling the tide that threatened to sweep her away into some anonymous whirlpool of annihilation, the best way she could. She never spoke about that time, not even how she met her husband … But something made Mansi feel, that whatever it was, that marriage was in a sense an act of desperation too, the way the elopement with Naresh was. The difference was that while that was an attempt to move on, this was an effort to find permanence, root herself to the earth.

She was reaching the other shore. The boat was just a little ahead of her now. She felt a pleasurable anticipation. At last the man would show his face. Maybe she would be able to talk to him … The boat slid on … came to rest with a jerk against the shore. Mansi put in a last spurt of effort. The man drew the oars in, rose up in the boat. He turned around … but … just then, the baby cried, waking her up.

The man is walking somewhere in the mountains. He paces through the woods with a swinging, easy stride. The road leads upwards, higher and higher. Mansi has left the lovely, fluid, formless lake behind and is toiling up after the man. On the firm, too-solid earth.

The baby is sound asleep now, but she can feel Saurabh pressing into her, making the man fade. Stop, stop, she wants to say. I want to see his face. But he presses deeper and deeper, clutches her milk-swollen breasts …

Mansi gives up. She'll never see the man's face … maybe … she doesn't want to any more … Did Nisha see any of their faces, examine them carefully? Perhaps she didn't want to either. But … if she had looked harder she might have found what lay behind them, and maybe something did, beyond what was obvious, in one of their faces at least. And if she had, perhaps the earth might have moved and carried her along in formless, fluid motion like the water, to some extraordinary, unknown plane of experience which transcended the present … to something better perhaps … who knew? But what was better—had Nisha herself found out? That constant swimming through the even current of her life, searching for the man who would not show his face. Never … ever … would the earth move for her either. But did she really want it to? She had yet to find out. Because she really didn't know what she would do if the earth should actually move.

It could be a disaster…

Doorways Without Doors

It stood halfway down the hill, just next to the spring which was supposed to have the best drinking water in the whole area. Not really a house, just a long narrow structure. A row of rooms with arched doorways—doorways without doors. Utterly decrepit, black with a coating of ancient moss, shelter for the poorest of the poor—a dharamshala.

Cacti sprouted from its roof, rampant, unchecked, stretching their prickly arms to the sky. An old *tun* tree spread benevolent branches over it, adding its own soft cover of fallen leaves to the carpet of moss that luxuriated atop the stolid slate roof.

Pragya wasn't sure why she had been so eager to come here. It had not been easy. Someone had blocked the old path that led down to the dharamshala from her house with thorns. Typically, it bolstered her determination, she had to get here at any cost. She had edged around the barrier, scrambled down an uneven slope, clutching at tufts of grass that provided a dangerously fragile hold, getting pierced with the very thorns she was trying to avoid and scraping a knee despite the frail protection of her cotton salwar.

In hindsight, it seemed rather silly to adopt this costume rather than a more practical pair of jeans if she had made up her mind to go slipping and sliding down the hillside,. But she was sensitive to the stares it might have provoked in this little town, who were unused to the sight of middle-aged women in pants, even though she chided herself for being a coward. Why couldn't she wear the clothes she had been wearing regularly for the last sixteen years? Why should coming home mean shrinking behind this flimsy armour?

But again, what compelled her to come scrambling down this impossible path? Nostalgia, a desire to get away from the sick room atmosphere, or just plain restlessness? Mamma had dozed off, there was a competent person—Abha— attending to her; more competent than she was perhaps, so she needn't feel guilty about taking a short walk, she had told herself firmly as she set off with the brittle April breeze stroking her cheeks. The pines murmured, imitating the music a sluggish rivulet might make. A sound so deceptive that it often induced visitors new to the place to enquire where the stream that they heard was flowing. The translucent warmth of the sunshine tempered the wind and despite the anxiety, the ennui of the past week, she experienced a sudden elation.

As a child she had sometimes come down here with her ayah for walks, or accompanied a servant to fetch water when the municipal supply let them down.

She found the place strange and curious then and would often hang back to peer into the ever-open doorways, scanning the darkness that prowled behind them, inhaling the peculiar odour that emanated from within. A compost of animal dung, scorched rice and damp, along with a generous hint of stale tobacco and unwashed bodies. Sometimes she would find an itinerant sadhu camped here, his eyes rolling redly, his matted locks inducing a strange prickling at the ends of her fingers as he puffed at his clay hookah. Only the fear of her ayah prevented her from going closer to touch them. More often, there would be a group of *dotiyals*, men from the north who worked as porters, dressed frugally in sackcloth with round caps perched on their heads. Sometimes muleteers stopped here for a night. They were responsible for the earthy odour of mule dung, which had become a permanent presence.

'Come on!' her ayah would admonish, her tough palms scraping Pragya's hand as she pulled her away. Pragya's fascination for this dilapidated place seemed to bother her. As if her charge of this middle-class child entailed keeping her away from such sights, apart from more clearly defined duties like bathing her, changing her clothes, taming her coarse, thick hair to make it lie flat and sleek on her small head, fetching the glass of milk to be drunk morning and evening. She would only agree to come down here when Pragya fussed so much in the course of the mandatory evening walk that she feared denial might result in an unpleasant scene—which could lead to adverse reports being passed on to Pragya's mother by inquisitive passers-by, this being a place where everyone knew everyone else.

But at a certain stage of her life, the ayah had left and as other forces intervened, the fascination had worn off, even though Pragya couldn't help glancing at the place curiously if she should ever happen to pass this way.

Some things had changed. The old house with the caved-in roof that used to perch on the slope overlooking the spring had disappeared. It had been replaced by a garish cemented edifice painted in unlikely shades of blue and green that clashed violently with both the sky overhead and the faded grass of the hillside behind it.

She remembered the story, extracted piecemeal from her reluctant ayah and further embellished by another more willing servant. The story of the woman who had once occupied that house, the do-gooder who constructed the dharamshala—a rani.

'Whose house is this?' She had asked the ayah, pointing at the dharamshala, the first time she brought her down here, a mistake Pragya knew she always regretted.

'Nobody's—everybody's,' the old woman had said. Her face was criss-crossed with as many wrinkles as the narrow paths that scored the hillside above and she smelled of the bidis she smoked surreptitiously.

'Is that why there are no doors?' Pragya asked. 'So that anyone can go in?'

'Yes,' the ayah nodded, playing along. At that time it seemed like a welcome distraction for this troublesome child, who wanted to run about here and there, leaving little time for the ayah to sit down and smoke her bidi in peace. 'If there were doors then there would be locks and everyone could not come and stay here. Only those who had keys.'

'But someone must have built it for everyone to stay here,' Pragya asked. 'Who?'

'A rani,' the ayah said. At that time she had been quite willing to talk about this place. It was before Pragya's obsession with it had begun to trouble her.

'A rani? Built this? This broken-down old house for everyone?' She had been disbelieving. What kind of queen would build something like this? A queen would build a palace—something grand.

'You're telling lies. You've made it up! I don't believe you!'

'It's true!' The ayah's tone matched hers. Sometimes they squabbled on an equal footing. Sometimes Pragya pushed her advantage, that of class and sometimes the ayah pushed hers, that of age. 'It wasn't broken down when she built it. She built it so that poor travellers could have a place to stay.'

'But why?'

'She wanted to perform a good deed. And now we're going home, it's getting dark. Your mother will get angry.' She had grabbed Pragya's hand and pulled her up the hill.

It was the servant who provided the rest of the story. He was not directly responsible for Pragya and when she followed him down to fetch water it was because no one else wanted to deal with her tantrums. Most of the other servants found it easier to let her have her way. So he did not bother to consider the consequences of answering the questions that flowed from her like the ayah did.

'Why did the rani build the house for travellers? Why did she want to do a good deed?' She had been watching the water trickle down from the spring, tamed into a channel, into the bucket, filling it soundlessly. The sun was strong that day and the stone enclosure which covered the spring—this water source that flowed eternally and never dried up even during the hottest of summers—felt deliciously cool. Quivering rods of sunlight executed a playful dance on its grey mossy walls and the damp air soothed her heated cheeks.

The servant had laughed. He had a soft full laugh which turned his eyes into slits, made his black moustache quiver. Then he sobered up suddenly. 'Because she was sick ... very sick ... she thought if she did a good deed she would get cured.'

'How silly! You can't get cured by good deeds,' she shot back at once. 'You have to go to the doctor if you're sick and take medicine.'

'Sometimes good deeds also help,' the man said shortly. 'And now we must go back because I have to cook lunch.'

She had paused to glance back at the house with its caved-in roof and fired one last question at him as she scrambled up the slope. 'Did she get better?'

The man paused too, before answering. 'I don't know.'

Somehow she had guessed that he was lying. Even then it had annoyed her that someone should try to fool her with stories, though beneath that annoyance an odd hope had lingered, that it could be possible. That good deeds could cure diseases or effect other miracles. Later, when she was much older and had totally lost interest in that dharamshala or anything else like it, she had once heard her mother tell a visitor about the spring, which gave the area its name, and the tubercular queen who eventually succumbed to her illness, despite all her good deeds. It was just another story, like the others that sprouted like grass on the hillside in her hometown.

It was just a few years before she met Vinay. She was in college at that time and the rani's story had not invoked much interest then, just that faint flicker which the answer to an old riddle might stir up. An answer that didn't seem relevant anymore because curiosity has evaporated long ago and been replaced by disinterest. At the most it provoked amusement at naïveté of this kind. She was living in a hostel in a big city then and had acquired all kinds of new knowledge and experience, far beyond what had been available to her in this little town. Visits home passed in a haze of ennui, which felt like a suspension of time that was spending itself despite the fact that everything seemed to be standing still; time that progressed just because clocks and calendars decreed it must rather than any effort on her part to move it along. Her father, her beloved Papa, was still alive then but her older brother Somesh had not gotten married as yet. That event would take place the following year and her father would pass away two years later, just when she was on the verge of completing her studies.

Papa's death had changed many things. She had learned to be afraid of the unexpected; an element of insecurity crept into that rather smug existence of hers. It had brought first disbelief, then anger that the force on which she had relied with such surety had suddenly withdrawn its favour from her, treated her like anyone else and finally implanted that fear into her heart—the fear which never left her for the rest of her life. Later it brought on the uncomfortable realisation that no one would be around to indulge her whims now, something she had begun to believe was her birthright. Her father indulged her so much that she took her status as a privileged being for granted. Someone who was special, born to be loved and have every wish fulfilled. Suddenly life came into brutal focus and she realized that she would have to take on another role, or rather experience a reversal of roles, be a kind of parent to the parent who remained, her mother, who had collapsed into a state of utter helplessness. She would be compelled to cosset Mamma's grief because her older brother had no interest in doing so, and despite her youth, her immaturity, slowly pamper, nurse it into a state of acceptance. But also into a state in which she, Pragya, became an essential prop to Mamma's existence.

When Vinay appeared on the scene he appeared to be the ally she badly needed in the mission to maintain her mother's well-being. The thought of a lifelong bulwark was so appealing that she surrendered to it right away. People had been surprised when she announced her engagement. Vinay was short, dark and beginning to show signs of a paunch at the age of twenty-seven. It was too much of a contrast to what people described as her ethereal beauty, despite his excellent qualifications as an engineer from a premier institute. But Mamma and Somesh were relieved. Because Vinay was so completely smitten that he was satisfied with the simplest of weddings, which was all they could afford at the time. And her confidence in this infatuation made it easy for her to disregard the displeasure, the coldness from the in-laws who felt cheated. There was someone who would indulge her again, like her father, and this belief gave her the strength to shore her mother up.

She didn't know at the time that the process of change that had set in with her father's death was still in motion. She realized it only when Vinay came and told her that he had made plans to leave the country. Without even consulting her. He had not thought it would be necessary—he was the decision maker and she the person who deferred to his decisions. It was only then that she realized that this bulwark was a wall built from her own illusions, her own needs.

'But your brother is there to take care of your mother,' he had said, bewildered at her protests. 'And you can visit whenever our finances permit.'

She stared at him dumbfounded, blinking back her tears, trying to make sense of his words. They had been married for more than a year, seventeen months to be exact. Shweta was just three months old. Her married life had so far followed the established pattern: the wedding, the honeymoon, the new house, furnishing which had been like creating the backdrop to an enchanted dream. And then the baby, the plump pretty daughter who, everyone had declared with approval, looked just like the mother. And now this, this incomprehensible decision to uproot them all, transport them to an alien place, far from all she cherished. How long had he been plotting and planning behind her back?

'But-but, why do we need to go?' she had asked. It was evening—that treasured time of day when he returned from office, weary but fulfilled. Another day of work, more money earned to keep his family in comfort, more security for them all. The time when he savoured his rewards, his blessings—playing with the baby, being pampered by Pragya. She had just served him a plate of hot onion pakoras, his favourites, when he asked her to turn off the gas and sit down. She misunderstood, thought it was love, an overwhelming desire for her company, which compelled him to make this request. She smiled and sat down on the sofa next to him, reached for his hand. Shweta was lying on a mattress on the floor, kicking her legs blissfully. Perhaps the fact that his responding smile was so fleeting should have alerted her.

At first she was not sure she had heard right. He had to repeat it again; 'I've got admission in a university in the US to do my PhD. I'm getting full financial support.' He had drawn a long, quivering breath and looked at her with shining eyes.

It had taken a few minutes for the words to register. Her first reaction was to quickly pull her hand away. 'You-you mean to say, you're leaving us, going away?' Tears streamed from her eyes.

'No, silly,' he grabbed her hand and squeezed it. 'How can I leave you? You'll join me later, as soon as I'm a little settled.'

'But-but, why do we need to go?'

'For a better future for us all.'

'But you never told me!' The words came out in a kind of wail, instead of the protest that she intended them to be.

He was silent for a moment. 'I wasn't sure it would work out. I didn't want to tell you till it was final.'

It did not take her long to realize how final it was. That the man who she had believed would be putty in her hands had an agenda of his own, had already had it when he met her. That what she believed was her duty to her mother did not enter into it, because he couldn't recognize it as such.

She had spent the eight months it had taken for him to get settled with Mamma, stoutly resisting her mother-in-law's commands that she come and stay with her. It was a form of revenge against Vinay.

All the same Mamma hadn't bothered to conceal the feeling of betrayal she experienced. Paradoxically, her reproaches, her nagging, made it easier for her to leave when the time came. The initial feelings of sorrow and guilt hardened into resentment. Why couldn't Mamma understand? Later she wasn't so sure. Was it the same resentment, which turned against Vinay later when he decided that he was not going to come home and work as he had said earlier? But she had come to terms with the facts of her existence and learned to rein in such feelings.

By that time Abha, the fourteen-year-old girl, had become firmly established with Mamma as a companion, helper, surrogate daughter, whatever.

Somesh and she had made a bargain. Mamma would spend winter with him. She would provide financial support to make her life more comfortable. Vinay had agreed to it. It was the bargain she made with him in turn, so that their lives could retain some semblance of their earlier wedded bliss. Later she had been able to send tickets for Mamma to visit when she herself couldn't, because after a time she too had found a job, created her own bulwark—a real one.

Mamma has been cared for, Pragya thinks, contemplating the doorless doorways of the dharamshala. She has even been able to transform a girl's life. Abha, the daughter of a drunken carpenter, has had the opportunity to go to school, to college, now even holds a well-paid job as a teacher, well-paid enough for her. She hasn't married, of course. If she had, who would have looked after Mamma? Somesh's wife, Lata, could not take on the responsibility. Mamma could be cantankerous, her demands were impossible to fulfil; even the three months that fell to Somesh's lot were a burden too great for them to bear. Luckily Abha, being a teacher, had holidays for part of those three months, even though Lata found it distasteful that she should use the guest room along with Mamma. But where else could she sleep? And what if Mamma needed something at night? Lata certainly didn't care to be disturbed.

And then, who would have married Abha? She had grown out of her class, would be hard put to adjust to someone of say, her father's level.

But now, Mamma's dying. Pragya knows that, hears it in the groans that keep her awake all night. Sometimes she sits up on her bed, her heart thumping uneasily. Is it coming, that awful moment? Sometimes she falls into an uneasy sleep in which Mamma's spirit seems to waft around her, touching her with vaporous fingers, cold as the mist outside. She awakes with a start to hear Mamma groaning again and is not sure if she should be relieved that her life drags on, however painfully. She wonders if she should go and see if she needs anything. Sometimes she does, only to see Abha seated there, bony-faced, silent, shaking her head when she asks if anything is required of her. Mamma does not groan all the time. Sometimes she seems to be delirious, reliving the past. She even repeats the story of the rani who died despite her battle, the ineffectual artillery of good works she had employed against death.

The story doesn't matter. There's a new twist that she discovered last night, though, through Mamma's ramblings. That the rani was young and beautiful and longed to live, was desperate to live. Does Mamma want to live, even though she keeps praying for deliverance? Is her life precious enough for her, lonely and neglected though she may consider herself? And unexpectedly, another thought intrudes. If deliverance should come ... what about Abha, what'll happen to her? The thirty-year-old schoolteacher who gravely performs her duty. The duty of which she will soon be relieved.

Sometimes she finds her in tears, this rather grim-looking young woman. She has performed her duty well, all these years, and developed a genuine attachment to Mamma, despite the fact that those demands had grown more and more difficult to fulfil as age and infirmity took their toll. There have been times that Pragya has argued with herself, wondering if she should be paid for these services. Somesh feels that what Mamma has done is more than enough. Food, shelter, clothes education ... could any other girl of her class have hoped to achieve what she has without Mamma's help? It's obvious Abha feels her position is above that of a servant's. A few years ago she stubbornly refused the tips Pragya tried to hand to her at the end of her yearly visit. After a couple of tries Pragya learned to substitute what she thought were reasonably decent gifts as part payment for the debt she sometimes feels she owes the girl, even though she knows it's not her fault she could not take care of her mother the way she should have. Even though Somesh is not conscious of any such lapse, she is fulfilling her part of the bargain as he is.

But Pragya lies awake at night subjecting herself to the torture of self-castigation. Hadn't Mamma been emotionally dependent on her? Can financial security stand in for the presence of a loved one, a child in one's old age? These are questions to which she can never find answers.

'If there had been doors, people would have been shut out ...'

'What doors? What are you talking about?' Somesh looks irritable.

Mamma is dead, the funeral is over. Now it's time to settle all those other mundane matters, tie up the loose ends left behind after someone's death—earthly possessions, clothes, furniture, property.

They sit in the verandah despite the evening chill, at her insistence. Inside, Mamma's missing presence is too strong. Somesh has agreed despite the fact that his wife has a cold. Perhaps because he's afraid that inside, Abha might eavesdrop. So they sit and watch the darkness congeal around them, braving the assaults the coming of night inflicts on them.

As Pragya makes her reply, Lata draws her shawl around her and sighs. 'I'm talking about the dharamshala down below, near the spring.'

Somesh clicks his tongue. Somesh, five years older, had already gone away to boarding school when she negotiated that rocky path with her ayah. 'What does that have to do with us?'

'What dharamshala?' Lata asks peevishly. Pragya knows how much she resents not being a part of their shared past, would blot it out totally if it were possible. Perhaps she'll manage to, now that Mamma's gone.

'Nothing really, perhaps,' Pragya delights in ignoring her. 'My mind was just wandering. Actually Mamma's mind wandered a lot lately. She was talking about the rani, the one who had built the dharamshala and died of tuberculosis … Sorry,' she sat up straight. 'I shouldn't digress. Yes, we have to decide what to do with the house, since neither of us is likely to come here much again.'

She felt a pang as she said this, seemed to hear a door slam which shouldn't have, a door that shut her out from something that had once been important to her life. But that was the way it had always been. Doors closing on compartments of her life, which sealed themselves up to become part of the jumbled storehouse of memory. Pathways blocked off with thorns. And soon she'd be hard put to scramble down that path again, stand face to face with the powerless magic of good deeds.

Powerless … Could it be called magic if it had no power? She thought of the rani … she hadn't really died as everyone believed but lived in the mossy walls of the dharamshala, floated in and out of the doorless doorways, along with the travellers who camped there. It was her scent she had been searching for so long ago, the scent of the person who constructed a shelter, however poor and decrepit.

No, death wasn't really a door slamming as she had thought.

'Yes, the house,' she repeated. 'I want to give my share to Abha. That's what Mamma would have wanted, wouldn't she? She did take on our burden.' She looked straight into Somesh's eyes as she said this, which dropped, to his credit. 'Perhaps she'll let me come and stay here sometimes ... And now I think I'll go inside,' she added, looking at Lata's shocked face as she rose and opened the door.

Maybe Mamma would remain here too, like the rani, and maybe she would understand that it wasn't really her fault, she thinks as she goes to find Abha.

House of Cards

She always lost, yet she continued to play. Why? She often asked herself. True, it sometimes gave her a kick to see his hard-earned money go down the drain. But there were times when she felt an unutterable, unbearable sadness overtake her—that she was so unlucky, even in cards. But the sadness strangely enough was as satisfying as the kick. Maybe because it was like an automatic, built-in punishment for her wickedness, cancelling it out, leaving her with a clean slate, a blank page in her copybook to blot all over again. What a worthless woman you are, she would tell herself, losing all your husband's hard-earned money. (Actually she was not a 100 per cent sure if it was really hard earned, but it felt better to tell herself so, honing the edge of the razor of guilt with which she wantonly lacerated herself, drawing blood in the form of tears) Often she went home and cried. Sometimes she couldn't even wait that long and, like a junkie desperate for her fix, began to cry in the car itself as she drove home—it made her feel better earlier. Sometimes if the tears were reluctant to come she actively encouraged them to. She thought of her empty purse and she thought of his anger when she asked him for more money and told him that she had lost again. She thought of her compliance that night when he put her through the routine. The days she lost she could actually enjoy it, while on normal days it nauseated her horribly.

Sometimes she got the feeling that he got a kick out of her losing too. That no matter how much he berated her, told her she was a worthless woman who was no good for anything, he got some kind of satisfaction too. As if her losses excited him in some inexplicable way. They definitely did. Didn't she know! He always coughed up, never refused to give her any more money, never told her to stop playing and he really enjoyed punishing her. She wasn't sure if she could stop playing but he never gave her the opportunity to find out. She didn't want to think about this too much. It confused her, diluted the feelings of guilt which were so important to her.

The day it happened—her adventure, that's what she liked to call it—she was really crying badly. She had lost a lot so the tears burst out the moment she left Minnie's house. Minnie's house was particularly unlucky for her. She always lost like mad even though she really loved Minnie's house, she'd done it up so well. Just the way she would have done up her own house if Rajat let her have the money. Funny, he never liked to spend too much money on the house, always said he was short when she wanted to redecorate. Anyway, she was barely able to restrain herself, didn't even wait to tuck into the wonderful spread Minnie had laid out. Minnie always did everything very well. She even won most of the time, small reasonable sums, not extravagant amounts which would have aroused envy and led to grumpy mutterings from people and snide remarks that she cheated.

She simply dashed out of Minnie's house, almost tripping over her trailing dupatta, desperately sniffing back the tears, scrabbling in her purse for the car keys, which seemed to have been hidden in some inaccessible corner as usual. Her tears almost blinded her as she started the car and began to drive down the road.

It was one of those dim winter evenings and people had already turned on their headlights. It was so foggy and smoky that she didn't bother to roll up the window. She felt absolutely sure that no one would notice the tears flowing down her cheeks in extravagant streams. She would have a headache by the time she got home, she knew. The thought gave her a dull satisfaction.

She had to stop at a red light. She was weeping really piteously by now and feeling absolutely wonderful about it, when a sudden impulse made her throw a quick glance to her side. She'd been overcome by that sudden creeping sense, that recognition of another presence that tells you that you're being watched. Sure enough she was. It embarrassed her a little. But by this time she was too far gone to stop. She couldn't, her tears had energy, a life of their own, they were beyond her control. So she looked straight ahead and continued to cry and feel the man continuing to watch her as if fascinated by this orgy of weeping. It was as if they were sharing something at that moment. She wasn't sure what but there was a communication of sorts. Then she thought she heard him say something. The words were indistinct and she wasn't even sure if she was imagining it all. In any case the lights changed just then and the cars behind her began to honk and she had to move on, half thankfully, half regretfully, because she was a little curious about what he was saying to her. A little confused too. He looked sympathetic, she thought. But she wasn't sure whether to feel happy or sad about it or whether it was good or bad that a strange man waiting at a traffic light next to her should react to her tears.

It's nice when someone looks sympathetic, of course. But when you've done something bad then it's not good at all, she knew. How can one sympathise with a wrong-doer? You need to punish them, and she really deserved to be punished that day. Not only had she lost heavily again but she had also left her poor little baby with the maid the whole day—the baby she was supposed to love and cherish but somehow didn't feel like a lot of the time.

All she wanted was the heady excitement of the card table and one enormous, mind-bending jackpot of a win. So she could take back a huge wad of notes and fan Rajat's face with it—or better still, strew them on the bed, pull off all her clothes and roll around in them naked, feel the sharp, crisp notes against her soft body. And then ... and then ... she would jump on him the way he jumped on her.

Yes, she was bad, bad, really perverted ...

And to crown it all, now she was pulling over to the side of the road because she had noticed that the car had been keeping close behind her.

Was the man following her? Would he stop? Would he ask her why she was crying? This was being impossibly bad, but she really wanted all this to happen. It was worth being bad so you could feel good when you were punished for it later on.

Sure enough, the car behind her stopped. And as she waited in the semi darkness, shivering, staring into her mirror, she saw a man get out and walk over. The footsteps rang deafeningly loud in her ear in spite of the clamour of numerous impatient horns blaring. Or was it her heart beating?

Her chest tightened so much as he approached that she felt she was about to explode, to burst into a thousand million fragments. 'Any problems ma'am?' he asked, leaning down to gaze at her through the half-open glass. His voice was as warm and soothing as toffee on your tongue. 'I was a little concerned. I could see that you were upset.'

A stranger ... concerned about her! That made her cry even more. But she wasn't sure whether it was good or bad. It was good to be sad, she knew, but she wasn't crying because she was sad. She was crying because his voice was so warm, so kind.

His stopping, stopping for her felt so good. As good as the sense of guilt that surged up when she remembered that she'd stopped deliberately. Just to see if he'd stop too.

When he spoke again his voice sounded alarmed—as if that torrential outpouring was not what he had bargained for. 'What—what's the matter?' he blurted out.

She said the first thing that came into her head. 'I'm sad.'

The man was silent for a moment. He had expected something more specific perhaps. Some tangible reason for grief, which would help him to offer a solution. But she felt it was an honest, straightforward answer. She *was* crying because she was sad. 'Anything I can do to help?' he asked uncertainly.

'Yes, make me happy,' she wanted to say, though the thought made her laugh inside. The sheer insanity of asking this poor good-hearted soul to make her happy. And maybe she did. Maybe a small giggle did escape her, because she noticed the way he started. But all she actually said was, 'Thank you, thank you,' sniffing into a disintegrating lump of tissue.

He peered at her uncertainly through the darkness as if not knowing how to continue. In a way he was trapped. Having stopped he could not just walk off even though she could already sense a kind of impatience with himself for getting into such an uncomfortable situation and with her for not giving him something substantial to work upon.

'I'll be all right, thank you so much,' she found herself saying again, her voice surprisingly steady now even though a sinking disappointment was taking hold of her.

The man would walk away, relieved. She would carry on home. The tears would keep on flowing till she had expended all her sadness, emptied herself of guilt and grief.

She would go home and tell Rajat that she had lost again. He would lose his temper, she'd bear it stoically—then would come the grand finale of her punishment. Though it was becoming more and more mechanically ritualistic—her wrongdoing, his anger, the punishment. A keen disappointment lanced her. She might as well as not have stopped at all if this was all that was going to happen.

'Thank you, thank you,' she repeated again softly, because the man still stood there, as if uncertain about what to do.

'Would you-would you like a cup of coffee or something?' he asked hesitantly.

A cup of coffee! Now that would be something really bad. Having a cup of coffee with a stranger. She felt a tingling in her crotch, felt her whole body clench into a knot of excitement. 'O-okay,' she sniffed. As if to show him that it was just the remedy for all her sadness.

Walking into the coffee shop of a five-star hotel, she felt exposed, naked in the bright light. She had thought of them going to a cosy, dimly lit place. He seemed to sense his mistake too, because he made an impatient sound.

'Is this-is this place okay?' he asked, looking into her eyes. He had rather nice eyes, warm and brown. In fact he was rather nice altogether. She had struck luck. 'Actually—I'm staying here ...' His voice trailed away, as if there was something he wanted to say but could not for some reason.

She said it for him. 'Maybe ... maybe we could go there—to your room—it would be more private. You know—just in case—' Just in case I start crying again was what she meant to say.

The sudden glint in his eye, the quickening of his breath spoilt it all. It showed that it was just not mere kindness that had led him to stop. Would he have stopped for an ugly woman?

Or did it really spoil everything? She felt confused. What did she really want from this stranger? If it was sympathy, which made her feel temporarily good, but guilty in the long run because she was bad, she didn't deserve sympathy, kindness. Punishment, expiation, these were things she understood better. But maybe in some twisted way he was doing her a kindness. Giving her an opportunity to be bad so she would deserve her punishment more. The punishment Rajat would definitely mete out when she got home late. She felt her own breath catch at the prospect. What a tremendous castigation it would be!

Funny how one got used to being hauled over the coals. How it became an essential part of one's life. Almost as necessary as breathing or eating. She thought of the punishments she had received in school as a child.

She had been sent to boarding school at the age of five, when her mother died. The memory of her first punishment remained vivid in her mind. She had knocked over a glass of water at the dining table. The standard punishment for this was a caning administered after dinner. She remembered the sick apprehension in the pit of her stomach. The horrible wait, the painful expectancy. The longing, longing for the moment to arrive so it could be over. The desperate wishing that some magic would make it vanish altogether. That Sister would have a sudden change of heart, would forgive her, would hug her and say it was all right.

Of course that didn't happen. And she could clearly recall the hard, tingling feel of the cane coming down on her hand. The sharp pain which stung tears from her eyes. And the relief ... the blessed relief when it was all over ... and she could retreat into herself, rubbing her aching hand and be thankful that her wickedness had been cancelled out. The slate was wiped clean ... and ... she could sin again.

She sinned often in many ways during the course of her school life. Perhaps they appeared to be petty misdemeanours when she thought of them now. At the time they were considered outrageous crimes—like dancing in the rain, eating wild berries or playing noughts and crosses in class. As she grew older her wrongdoings became more heinous—like trying to jump over the school wall to go and see a movie, writing a letter to a boy etc. It was not that she did it deliberately. It just seemed to happen on its own. Maybe she was just born to be bad. It was in her genes perhaps. But then, there was something she felt pretty smug about—she never shirked her punishment. She paid for whatever she did. And that made it all right.

Later, when she passed out from school, Dad took over the responsibility of punishing her from the sisters. And the first time he did it, it was horribly painful too. The same sharp, piercing pain, like the cane coming down on her hand. No, a hundred times sharper and more painful. But it became a little confusing then. It was hard for her to pinpoint her offence. Sometimes she felt she was being punished for no reason at all, just for existing, maybe. And perhaps that was reason enough for Dad. She was thankful at least to be able to do something that seemed to give him some kind of satisfaction. But she was not too sure about that even. Because he invariably wept when it was all over. He even begged her forgiveness at times. That made her cry too. Worse, it made the punishment seems less of one. Because aren't the righteous meant to chastise the wicked?

'Why are you sad?' he asked, looking at her curiously with those bright brown eyes. They were sitting in his room. A typical, pleasantly-decorated, characterless hotel room. Perhaps just the right setting for this bizarre interlude. He had ordered coffee from room service for her and poured out a drink for himself.

'I'm sad ... because I'm bad,' she said. Then giggled because of the silly rhyme it made.

He laughed too, thinking it was a joke. 'But seriously,' he asked. 'Why were you crying?'

'Because I lost at cards ... I'm always losing at cards. Squandering my husband's hard-earned money ...'

He stared at her for a moment with those lovely, serious, honey-brown eyes. 'Then why don't you stop playing?'

'I can't. Don't you see? I can't!'

'I'm sure you can if you really want to.' He looked really earnest when he said that. She felt like smiling. How innocent he was. As if life was that simple!

'I'm not sure that I want to ...'

'Then why cry?' he looked exasperated now.

She was silent for a moment. Then, feeling that he deserved an explanation because he had, after all, made a serious effort to help her, even if there were some ulterior motives involved, she said, ' I like to play cards. In fact I'm crazy about it. But I always end up losing as I told you ...'

'And your husband—what does he say?'

'He gets angry! He punishes me. But he always lets me have the money.'

'Punishes you? How does he punish you?'

She dropped sugar cubes into her coffee, stirred them, felt them dissolve in the liquid—like the heat of punishment dissolved her guilt, absorbed it. She looked up at him, ran her tongue over her lips. 'He has ways,' she said with a suggestive smile, and giggled.

Bright sparks shot out of his eyes, scorched her. He gazed at her for an endless moment. She felt herself melting, liquefying inwardly. 'Shall I—shall I punish you today?' he asked, his voice hoarse.

That made her think. Why should he, a total stranger, punish her? How had she wronged him that he should mete out chastisement? Punishment had to be earned ... But then ... How had she wronged Dad? And he had still punished her ... How he had punished her. He had only stopped when Rajat took over.

'All right,' she said. 'Go ahead. Punish me ...'

She couldn't even wait, and began to undress right away, she was that impatient. Because a sudden unbearable excitement surged up within her. Rajat would have even more reason to penalise her tonight. This—this was probably worse than playing cards. Much, much worse. What a stroke of luck, finding this man!

Her mobile trilled as the last shudders of bliss were dying away. 'Coming, just coming, darling,' she murmured, as smooth as honey in the face of Rajat's anger. It promised so much!

Tonight would be the mother of all punishments ...

Babies

If there's one thing Nalini loves, it is babies. She loves the way they pop out, all covered with birth slime, perfect little beings (actually not always, sadly), but perfect all the same just because they are there, miniature men and women, drawing breath—and all because of her. The thrill she experiences when she hears the first thin wail of a new-born, sees it kick its tiny legs, cannot be compared with anything in the world. Her juniors have strict instructions to call her well before the infant makes its entry, unlike many senior gynaecologists who appear only if there are serious complications, or barely in time to formally record the delivery.

And those frenzied moments before the actual birth! The last desperate contractions, the mother's drawn-out scream and the sheer supernatural force that propels a baby out, a frantic swimmer, tearing its way into life. Nalini revels in them.

Of course, it doesn't always happen like that. There are caesareans, deliveries with forceps, and other painful complications. But whatever the method, the moment of nativity holds such pure magic that at times she wants to burst into a paean of thanks to the power that made it so, and to bow her head in gratitude that she's been permitted to participate in this wonderful, enchanting process.

She has a whimsical habit. She insists on having each baby she's delivered photographed, and keeps a copy of the photo. The photos are mounted in a particular way. She has fashioned an enormous collage with her own picture at the centre and the babies radiating out from it. It hangs directly opposite her bed, so it can be the first thing she looks at in the morning, and the last at night.

Her husband Jayant, an equally successful psychiatrist, doesn't feel the same way, alas. The first hint she got was a few years ago, when he told her teasingly that she should not celebrate contributing to the population explosion.

The collage had almost obliterated one wall of their bedroom by then.

Hurt that he was unable to appreciate her sentiments, she had said, 'They're my babies. I want them close by.'

Deliberately ignoring the agitation contorting his smooth-featured face, she had smiled and patted his cheek, even though the dim echo of an almost forgotten pain thrummed through her body. Ironically, while helping two babies into the world, she had lost her own. A long day's work had resulted in a miscarriage. After that, for all their trying, she had been unable to conceive. She had resisted Jayant's suggestion that they adopt a child. It felt like putting the seal on her own inability to bear one, owning up to the world that she was barren. Which she knew she wasn't. How could she be? Didn't she deliver a baby almost every day?

And now … the babies were happily sprawling all over the four walls of her bedroom, leaving just a few square yards of beleaguered space.

The other day Jayant, during one of their rare moments together, made another attempt. 'What will you do when the walls are filled up?'

'Start another on the ceiling.' She could see Jayant's eyes expand behind his glasses. He crossed and uncrossed his long legs, then jerked up from the easy chair. She could almost guess what he was thinking—that soon the whole house would be taken over by the babies. The rate at which she produced them made it quite possible.

Why not, she thought, ignoring the comment muttered under his breath as he walked away—'You're crazy!'

Seated on the top floor of her three-storeyed mansion, the dream maternity home she has slaved to achieve, in plangent, echoing solitude, Nalini smiles again, recalling Jayant's dismay. Why can't he just enjoy the babies on the wall, and the others, wailing, suckling, wetting their diapers in the rooms below? Then she glances at her watch. It's 10:45. Has he come back? She rises and peers out of her window into the dim January night. Her bedroom overlooks the gate and it's hard to make out if his car is standing in the driveway, closer to the main door. She experiences a minuscule twinge of unease. Driving on a smoggy winter night in Delhi can be risky at times.

Occasionally, he slips into his room without a word to her. He doesn't want to disturb her, he says. It's her practice to go to bed early, get some sleep in case she has to get up in the middle of the night to deliver a baby. Her uncertain schedule makes it almost impossible for them to make plans together, and they have slowly come to accept that Jayant will have to seek his evening entertainment alone. Because babies do not recognise clocks. *They* decide the moment of their entry into the world. And Nalini respects that. She scorns those doctors who hurry things up with a caesarean if they have movie tickets.

Tonight, however, she's up late because there's a patient whose labour has progressed so far that she can expect to be called down any moment. Nalini's eyes dart to the collage again, and the taut lines of her angular face soften. The faint disquiet she feels, speculating on Jayant's whereabouts, vanishes.

The very next minute she starts, hearing a familiar knock on the door.

'Anamma?' The sight of her head nurse brings a spurt of the cherished anticipation.

'They've taken number eight—Rina—to the delivery room, madam.' Anamma's even face, precisely contained within her starched white cap, is calm. 'The intercom isn't working, so I came up.' Dear Anamma. Never flustered.

'Let's go!' Nalini's voice turns brisk. Approvingly, she notes that Anamma has already picked up the camera that lies ready on her dressing table.One of the new digital kinds. Jayant gifted it to her on her last birthday.

'You can store your photos on the computer,' he had said.'On a CD too. You can look at them any time you want.'

'It won't be the same.' Nalini's lower lip had thrust itself out.

Jayant's eyes had acquired that alien gloss, and he had quickly backed into his own room.

She remembers Anamma's remark, made a long time back. 'Madam, why is *saar* sleeping in another room?' Then almost under her breath, 'It's not good.'

'It's more convenient,' Nalini had snapped.

Anamma's face had shrivelled. Remorse clawed at Nalini, forcing her to launch into an explanation. Anamma was more than just a mere employee, at times Nalini ached to make her a confidante. 'He gets disturbed when there's a case at night.'

It *was* her suggestion, that Jayant and she occupy separate rooms, to avoid waking him up when the summons came at an odd hour. Even though it hurt terribly that she could not share that excitement with him—that burst of adrenaline that suffused her when she learned that another birth was imminent. And when she returned after the event, she was so charged up that she *had* to talk about it. In the beginning she would, in minute detail, describe the procedure she had used, the appearance of the baby, the mother's response. But once she discovered that he had dozed off in the midst of her animated talk. She had felt pained, offended, disappointed. Later, however, she had turned contrite—that she had been so full of herself, she had not realised he was tired. That she hadn't understood it was impossible for him to react the same way to the coming of the babies.It was different for a man. Then she thought of the expectant fathers, some were so overcome that they burst into tears. But how could she compare them with Jayant?

They had managed to perpetuate themselves, were reaching out towards immortality. A tiny version of them was entering the world; their seed could go on replicating itself till eternity. And she was seized by the most awful guilt.

The birth is a routine affair. A first child, a healthy boy. The family rejoices.

Returning to her room, Nalini notices the sliver of light under the door of Jayant's room. It's past two. Why is he up so late? But she can't wait to print out the new photograph and add it to the collage.

Only when she slips into bed and is drawing the pink satin quilt over herself does a bothersome vagabond of a thought creep into her mind. Has he just gotten home? Where had he been? But sleep is assailing her in powerful waves, and drowns the thought out.

That night she has a strange dream. She's flying out of her bedroom window, trying to catch hold of a baby that has detached itself from the collage and floated off.

'Come back!' she cries. 'Come back where you belong!'

The baby turns and winks. To her dismay, she discovers that it has Jayant's face. And as she gazes at it, astonished, a host of chortling, babbling babies suddenly materialize behind her with a loud whoosh. They fling themselves into the sky like disobedient balloons that have torn themselves loose from their anchoring strings, and grow smaller and smaller till they vanish altogether.

Nalini wakes up, her heart stuttering painfully, her body damp with sweat, despite the January cold. After an indecisive interval, her hand creeps to the bedside table, seeking the switch to the lamp. The room is awash with hesitant light, which seeks out and defines the numerous small shapes on the collages all around her.

Her babies are safe!

Nalini's hands fold themselves over her heart as a juddering sigh brings a welcome torrent of warmth to her body. She lies like that for a long time, inert, gazing at her babies.

She had not been strictly truthful with Anamma, about why it was more convenient to have separate bedrooms. A time had come when she couldn't share this space with anyone but her babies. And safely glued down as they are, locked up in the computer too now, with backups on CDs, they will never fly away from her.

Let Jayant roam where *he* will.

Why Did You Kill Mahatma Gandhi?

Possibilities are endless, and thought a river ever flowing. But reality is inescapable too … and therein lies the rub.

Mrs Lal looked at the grass, the green of the trees outside. A tiny, creeping excitement bubbled and bloated inside her. The leaves were so unbelievably green. So unnatural, a miracle in this city of dust and grime.

It was as if someone had been up and about, cleaning, polishing them specially for her. Yes, there was something to be said in favour of sickness. Everything looked new, different. She hadn't felt so alive, so charged with energy for ages. Now she felt clean, new and whole, ready to take on anything. Cleaning cupboards, cooking an extra-special meal, starting on that exercise schedule—so essential and yet so often postponed. They all felt like extraordinarily exciting things to do! And of course, how could she forget, buying material for new sofa covers. She wrinkled her nose, (rather short, a little broad but quite attractive all the same) as she looked at the grubby, discoloured shapes before her. Receptacles for people to lower their backsides into. To recline, lounge, sit upright, or perch nervously at the edge. Or wipe their greasy fingers on, nonchalantly, indifferently, furtively, overcome with pangs of guilt, perhaps. She would make them fresh and new like herself, make everything fresh and new in her life.

And then, as unexpectedly, dissatisfaction clamped itself onto her, a damp, fat wave, an irritable mist blotting up her ebullience. Trust herself to think of sofa covers instead of letting that wonderful, rare exhilaration carry her off to something different and momentous. Something that could transform her—from this shapeless lump in the not-so-new sari with toe nails that needed to be trimmed, somewhat like one of the sofas opposite her—into someone quite different.

Not someone who just cleaned cupboards and cooked extra-special meals and for whom an exercise schedule was something revolutionary. She saw herself opening up like Chinese boxes and a series of Monisha Lals emerging for her to pick which one she wanted to be. Yes, she could even choose to be a mini-skirted person with purple hair, someone who would not nod benignly and just tap her foot when music played but would dance, dance, dance with wild abandon. Whoorf! It made her breathless just to think about it. But, as always, spoilsport reality interposed and she saw the Chinese boxes closing in on themselves and shutting up, confining the dancer, the adventurer, the buccaneering entrepreneur—all those possibilities—deep within that crevice inside her, that magical cave, where they'd always lived.

How rooted one got! How impossible it was to take flight! Sometimes she felt small, incipient wings beating inside her, watching TV programmes with people, going off to exotic destinations, setting off on dangerous expeditions, braving discomfort, bug bites, bad food, going without a bed, tea and proper meals (dal, subzi and roti for her). How did people manage without the kind of food they were used to? She couldn't even stand visiting relatives, where the tea didn't taste the same, the phulkas were not cooked to the right consistency and where the pillows didn't feel the same. She could never get a decent night's sleep away from home. But all the same she longed to be able to dash, zoom off at a moment's notice, arrive at some impossible destination with a happy face and a smile for the camera. And here she was, such a firm fixture, such a well-fitting round peg in a round, permanent hole, made to measure for people like her.

The saddest fact was, no one could ever dream that she could even harbour such fancies. Worse, surely no one could believe or imagine that she had ever been young—a frolicsome, lively child even. In fact, she'd almost forgotten it too.

A little girl in a frilly frock and a ribbon in her hair. Quite a cute child if you looked at her childhood photographs. Black and white, of course, sometimes a little out of focus. But one could make out that she had been a pleasant-looking child.

She remembered her older brother's friend. What was his name? It had escaped her—permanently, perhaps. She couldn't even recall his face. Odd, he was always at their house. She recalled only the peculiar question he used to ask her—'Why did you kill Mahatma Gandhi?'

What a thing to ask a six-year-old child! But it was one of those quirky, nonsensical things boys liked to do—to tease, provoke, build up a crazy exasperation in someone younger, someone easy to scare and confuse.

She remembered her frantic denial. The sickness, the terror squeezing her belly. The feeling of guilt, irrational though it was, lodged in her like a speck of grit in her eye, which couldn't, wouldn't be blinked out even though she wept streams of tears.

'No! No! I didn't!' she'd cried, her voice going higher and higher.

'Yes, you did,' he'd whispered. 'I know you did, admit it.' His eyes had fixed themselves on her—round, glassy, accusing. She'd trembled, her lower lip had curled like a baby's, she hadn't been able to control herself.

'No-no!' she'd quavered, beginning to whimper now. Her mind raced ahead contemplating all the horrible possibilities. She could see the police coming, the handcuffs, the bars of the cell and ... the noose.

At six she had been aware of these possibilities. She even knew who Mahatma Gandhi was, and understood the heinousness of the crime ascribed to her very well.

'No!' she'd screamed. Their laughter had saved her. Danger, terror, became a joke as she stared at their faces, all flashing teeth, bulging cheeks and crinkled eyes. She felt bewildered at first, then the speck in her eye melted away. Or did it entirely? A tiny atom remained. The seed of fear, almost invisible. So did a kind of perverse self-importance. She, Monisha, little Monu, as they called her—all of six years old—had been considered capable of killing Mahatma Gandhi. A big, important man, whose picture was everywhere. The absurdity of it all did cast a film of doubt, clouded that importance. But—they had said it, hadn't they?

And that accusation, so outrageous, so disproportionate, hummed in her mind, filling her with quasi-murderous intent, making her scare her little brother by yelling, 'I'll kill you!' and by playing at throttling him till he screamed in turn and her mother came to separate them.

'What's wrong with this girl?' she had said. 'Has she gone mad?' That had opened up another line of thought. She was no longer a possibly murderous but a mad little Monu. And being mad gave you some kind of license, she knew.

It wasn't a good thing to be mad. But certain activities did require a kind of madness. Had she really possessed it once, or had she just imagined she had? It was hard to be sure. She had never explored that possibility enough.

But there was one thing she was sure of. No one would dream of asking her now, 'Why did you kill Mahatma Gandhi?' And she knew she should be thankful for it, because it would definitely imply some modicum of insanity or a taste for particularly sick jokes in the questioner.

They could only ask, 'What's for dinner?' or 'Why hasn't the maid removed this cobweb?' or 'Where should we go this holiday?'

And if she replied, 'Boating down the Amazon,' her husband would probably smile and say, 'Sure, let's—what a wonderful idea.' But just a few minutes later he would continue without even changing his expression, 'If we have to go to Goa this winter, we must make the bookings now.'

And her own mind would work itself into a frenzy, computing costs, air fare, hotel stay, transport, meals and want to abandon the whole project in despair, thinking of all that money being blown up, their nest egg depleted, her bastion of security weakened. And she'd say, 'Need we go that far? Won't it be better to go somewhere closer? Bharatpur, for instance?'

Her husband would look relieved and say, 'Yes, why not? That's a better idea. I really can't get away for long.'

And she'd relax too. But yet remain dissatisfied. As if she'd tightened another knot. A knot of safety securing her safely within herself—or a noose, slowly tightening around her neck, not letting her breathe. Not letting her gulp in huge mouthfuls of invigorating, energising oxygen, which might even enthuse her to actually attempt all those extraordinary things she could only dare to dream about. But as she sank deeper and deeper into the morass of middle age, she shut her eyes to the allure of the rain forest, the squawking birds, the stealthy, dangerous beasts, and abandoned the chance to be a weather-beaten woman in jeans (broad-beamed but tough as they come) who braved the piranha-infested waters of the Amazon or the snowy, impossible heights of the Himalayas.

Well, this was life, she thought rather droopily—suddenly no longer inclined to clean cupboards or begin an exercise schedule. What for? She was not a young bride who had to prove her housekeeping skills to her in-laws, she was not even interested in being slim and desirable any longer. It was not appropriate now—not even worth the trouble. Yes, that was another thing denied to her now. She could not dare to try and look attractive. She would not be able to face the mockery of her peers—the over-ripe ladies she met at kitty parties, mechanically playing tambola or munching samosas with avid greed, their gimlet eyes assessing the value of her jewellery or the diamond tops she had acquired, not out of any great desire for them but as a necessary adjunct to her station in life.

But the grass, the grass, the shiny waving leaves outside! They remained so exotically verdant. It was real, that extra-special brilliant green, that bright, impossible dimension. She wanted to feel, experience that gloss, that colour, that freshness from close. She remembered how she used to lie, roll, in the grass, inhale its sweet scent, chew on a juicy stem. She had climbed trees too. She could remember the hard scabby trunks, the branches, the exhilaration of being high up above the ground. If only she could become a bird perched on a tree surrounded by nothing but leaves. If only ... she could float off, free herself from these lumpy anchors, the heavy shapeless sofas weighing her down, rooting her to the earth ...

But I'm too heavy, she thought. The branches will snap ... there's no tree that can hold me up now.

But the branches didn't snap ... though the leaves were not so green from close. It was not that comfortable either. The scabby bark bit into her behind and there were ants. A spider swung perilously close to her nose. 'Shoo! Shoo!' she cried, batting at it with her hand. As if it could hear. Could it? Could spiders hear, understand human talk. Would it understand if she shouted out, '*I* killed Mahatma Gandhi! *I* killed Mahatma Gandhi!'

Of course, she hadn't killed Mahatma Gandhi. The spider knew. But she didn't know, hadn't been sure, the day he had come upon her alone. He hadn't been laughing then. His eyes had been round and glassy as ever and his voice had hissed in her ear. 'I know it. I know you killed Mahatma Gandhi.'

'N-no,' she had stammered. 'I-I didn't.' She was utterly bewildered. She had thought that chapter closed. Several days had passed since that incident, though at times her older brother did tease her sometimes, saying, 'Why did you kill Mahatma Gandhi?'

'I didn't, I didn't,' she would reply, mechanically playing along, but not disturbed.

But today she was. More than disturbed. Fear had crawled up her arms and taken possession of her heart. It had banged and thumped at her from there, making her lips stiff, her mouth dry, her breath short as he clambered up the tree to sit next to her.

'Yes—you did ...' He had fixed her with his gaze. Try as she might she could not pull her eyes away. When he said, 'You will have to be punished ...' it was almost a relief. She would do anything to escape that nameless, creeping terror. If she expiated, the guilt would be cancelled ... if the guilt could be cancelled, the terror would go away ... That's why she didn't mind it at all. Didn't mind that hand coming down, hot and hard against her bare behind, didn't mind what followed either ...

The cool green leaves had suddenly been spattered with mud. As if the unknown somebody who had been polishing them for her had decided to muddy them again in a fit of perversity.

Funny she couldn't remember his face or his name. He had left the town soon after when his father was transferred. She had been thankful. Her terror on beholding him had become a joke, though, for her brother. She had fled whenever she caught sight of him from afar. She did not want to be punished again. Because the guilt hadn't gone, nor the terror. She had never been quite sure that she hadn't killed Mahatma Gandhi ...

Visitor's Hour

The hands of the little clock on her desk have crept past the 5:30 mark this January evening, but Nitya hasn't noticed it. It's the announcements on the public-address system that alert her to the fact that it's visitor's hour. A misnomer actually, because visiting time at the girls' hostel stretches on till 8:30 for male guests. Women can visit this rectangular structure throughout the day—three floors of nondescript rooms housing female students at the university. Then the gatekeeper, endowed with an air of righteous authority, shoos out all those who linger in the long airless lobby, where visitors perch on scuffed faux leather settees, examining the boards on which the names of the former office bearers of the hostel are painted, while they wait. It's mostly parents or other elderly relatives who occupy these seats, with impatience or fortitude according to their respective temperaments. Middle-aged women, their red bindis brightening their faces, their gold bangles tinkling as they gesture, sharing desultory conversation with their male companions. Boyfriends tend to stand around like eager, chafing horses or stroll up and down on the straggly patches of grass outside.

The announcements reach her ears like scratchy music from a distant loudspeaker, a sound that her brain registers but does not consider worth deciphering. Her eyes remain glued to her book and her mind is a resolute wall shutting all distractions out. The assignment has to be handed in tomorrow and twenty-two-year-old Nitya is serious about her work. And then she knows there's no chance of her getting any visitors. She is a local and there would be no occasion for her mother or brother to visit even if they had the time. Mamma is not the type to go in for such frivolous surprises and her younger brother, Akshay, who might be inclined to visit, is too busy cramming for his board exams. He's also taking extra coaching to be a worthy competitor for the various entrance tests which will follow—those magic keys to the enchanted world of success, on the door of which they have been knocking long and hard.

In any case, she goes home almost every other weekend, traversing the streets of Delhi in a bus, indifferent to the clamorous rush of traffic. She hates to admit it, but apart from the desire to bond with Mamma and Akshay, a despicable weakness is another powerful draw: her mother's cooking. She hates the hostel food, the discomfort of cramped accommodation, of having to share common toilets, and has long dithered between the options of living at home or the hostel. But it's not just that she would have to travel a long distance to college each day. There's something about the neutral, detached world of the hostel that makes her feel at peace despite the inconveniences. There's a certain unidentifiable stability in this dispassionately regulated way of life. She had used the excuse that she could concentrate better on her studies if she moved here. Maybe it was true. And, possibly, some instinct has prompted her to use this experience as a breaking-in process for the final break which will come soon—when she leaves home to create her own life.

But both Mamma's cooking and Mamma have become more erratic than ever. There are days when she is effusive and loving, serving up all of Nitya's favourite dishes, leading Akshay to exclaim, the last time she had done it, 'Hey, you better not miss a single weekend, Didi. At least I get some decent food for a change.'

She had swallowed the gasp that had whooshed up her throat, thrown a quick apprehensive glance at Mamma. But instead of flaring up as Nitya had feared, Mamma had laughed and ruffled Akshay's hair, probably because she knew he hated it, and said, 'I better give you some bad food for a change, so you have a real reason to complain.'

Then she had flung her straggling dupatta over her shoulder and walked to her room with deliberate slowness. A little later, the odour of sandalwood had drifted out, followed by the tinkling of a bell. Mamma's evening devotions—a regular worshipper, she was lighting incense, chanting prayers. But Nitya's mouth had turned acrid as she visualized her smart career-woman mother, head reverently veiled, supplicating an indifferent deity.

Nitya is busy writing away in her notebook when the door is pushed open roughly. It's her roommate Soma, who'd gone to pick up some snacks from the canteen. She can't study, she says, without something to munch upon. Her angular face is furrowed with irritation; her tiny diamond nose stud glints sharply. 'Have you gone deaf?' she complains. 'They've been announcing your name for the last ten minutes.'

'Announcing my name?' Nitya's full, soft mouth hangs open.

'Don't look so surprised. You've got a visitor.'

Something in the way Soma says this fills Nitya with unease. But she knows it won't be any use asking her to explain. Soma takes a perverse delight in posing riddles, not providing answers till you're so exasperated that you're not sure you want to know any longer. The only way to end the suspense is to go down as fast as she can and find out who it is herself.

She runs down the pitted grey cement stairs without even bothering to comb her dishevelled hair or change her shabby, shapeless cardigan, doesn't even pause to think that at home Mamma would never have let her appear before a visitor like that. At the entrance to the lobby, she halts for a moment to examine the bunched-up groups deep in conversation. But she can't see anyone she knows. Could Soma have been mistaken? Only when she hears her name being called out does she recognize the familiar voice. Her breath catches; reluctantly her eyes swivel around to clash with his.

It's the toupee that has confused her. She should have experienced revulsion, disgust, but feels nothing but embarrassment that she couldn't recognize her father, even though it's been a while since she has seen him. Self-castigation follows and then a wry amusement. It's in keeping with the persona that he has assumed ever since he left them—this startlingly younger-looking man whom she has known as her father. A kept man needs to pay attention to his appearance and probably doesn't need to maintain the façade of dignified authority expected of a father with grown-up children, especially a father with a daughter of marriageable age.

Despite herself, she can't help exclaiming, 'Papaji!' Then she glances around to see if anyone's watching.

His sheepish smile makes crows' feet fork out on his temples, and he looks old again. He comes forward briskly to mask the awkwardness, but something quivers in the corner of his mouth. She forces herself to think of Mamma—her brittle laugh, the chain-smoking, the time she found her sitting all alone in the drawing room staring at nothing when she got up to get a glass of water at night—but it doesn't work. That barrier crumbles, inexplicably. There's a tearful gratitude in the way she allows herself to be embraced (later she's going to hate herself for it), inhaling the familiar scents—his cologne, the harsh odour of his tweed coat. A new one she notes, withdrawing. His girlfriend treats him well, she thinks, and the unbidden thought causes something to close up, clamp her chest with chilly bands of steel. The fleeting moment of joy flees along with her smile.

But he doesn't seem to notice. It's enough perhaps that she has received him without obvious animosity. 'What's happened to your contact lenses? Why are you looking like such a studious type? And so thin too. Doesn't your—' He stops himself in time, covers up by saying, 'Don't they feed you here?'

Her smile returns, though much diminished. 'When did you come?' she asks instead of answering. Maybe such questions are just rhetorical. He doesn't live in Delhi anymore and this is only the third time she has met him since he left two years ago, sneaking out of the house to go and live with his rich girlfriend.

Funny, she thinks, in a way it was a relief when he actually left. Not that there were scenes, quarrels, or any ugliness between her parents before that. But, unlike Akshay, she had been able to sense something deep and hidden behind those silences. Something more than the common displeasure that had caused her parents to stop talking to each other for days on end earlier. Or had she really? Perhaps all she been aware of was the discomfort that that plangent, disquieting silence had caused her and instinctively blamed him for it. And that, perhaps had opened her ears to the whispering, the meaningful glances of neighbours and relatives.

How long had those silences existed? She wasn't too sure. Mamma had always been quiet; he was the one for words. Strangely, though, Mamma had opened up after he left, had become almost verbose, as if someone should fill the empty space he had left behind.

He answers the question she is not inclined to ask, not out of fear of unpleasantness, but inexperience of such meetings. She does not have any friends who have estranged fathers. Her quick, keen eyes have not had the opportunity to observe the niceties of such social encounters. Perhaps she should have used this opportunity to punish him, as he deserves, hand out the tongue-lashing that is his due. But like Mamma she hates loud voices and angry words, and would rather sacrifice the pleasure of putting him down than face that unpleasantness. 'I came here for some work and couldn't leave Delhi without seeing you, at least,' he says.

'Do you hate him?' Soma had asked. It was one of those nights when, lying awake in the stuffy little room, the proximity, the darkness and the stillness of the night had coaxed them into letting those hidden thoughts flow, thoughts they hid so assiduously in the light of day, when both she and Soma seemed like different people, so confident, so much in command of themselves. So seductive was the allure of letting everything flow out in that dimness that many a time she had had to exert all her will power to rein in those runaway thoughts.

All the same, she had answered Soma truthfully, as she stared at the faint outline of the fan whirring above her, as if it would help to make that dilemma clear in her mind. 'It's funny, but I don't.'

Soma's reply, 'That's strange, yaar, but you're a very tolerant person,' filled her with unease.

No, I don't, she tells herself again, looking at the short blunt nose she has inherited from him, along with the full mouth. Perhaps it's because suddenly she's not so sure. 'Don't you want to see Akshay too?' she hears herself ask. It's a natural response to his statement. If he can't leave Delhi without seeing her, it's natural that the same sentiment would apply for her brother. Mamma wouldn't mind she knows, but she's not too sure about Akshay. His anger is enormous, such a huge, swelling wave that sometimes it threatens to engulf them all. He has never made any attempt to hide it either, even if it were possible for him to do so. Being a girl, or perhaps just being practical by nature, she has learned to stopper emotions which create nothing but frustration or lead to pain greater than the initial agony, even though this kind of capitulation sometimes fills her with shame.

'Do you need anything?' he asks.

Not really, she wants to reply. Mamma's job pays reasonably well, their needs are few and simple, and they are definitely not in want. But with a shock she discovers a strange greed forking up—a greed so strong and overwhelming that she cannot control it. She shrugs, smiles piteously and glances away. 'Oh … no, not really …'

He rises to the bait and quickly counts out five thousand rupees from a wad he produces from his pocket and stuffs it into her hand with guilty haste. The notes feel stiff and harsh against her palm and crackle faintly as her fingers close over them. She does not have a purse in which she can place them so she lets her taut hand fall clumsily into her lap.

'Is it enough?' he asks, anxious lines etching themselves on his face.

She nods with an artificial, awkward smile, notes the way his eyes cloud.

To her astonishment he quickly counts out four more five hundred-rupee notes. Her palm feels stuffed to bursting now.

'Have fun,' he says, stretching his mouth as far as it can go. 'This is the time to enjoy life.'

Confounded, she can only nod.

'Is Akshay studying hard for his exams?'

'Yes, Mamma's made him join coaching classes. I'm sure he'll do well. He's determined.' She prattles on. 'I'm going to be through this semester. I've already got a placement—in a firm in Mumbai. Mamma thinks I ought to get married but I want to concentrate on my career right now. I think it's more important. Don't you?'

She pauses to glance at him. He hasn't responded with more questions but is examining the grimy floor intently. Perhaps he hadn't bargained for so much information. Perhaps he's not really interested in her—their plans. He's wearing nice shoes, she notices, suede, a sort of greyish-brown. His clothes are definitely more stylish now. Maybe she, his girlfriend, likes him to dress well, buys him clothes. Mamma didn't really care.

He startles her by saying suddenly. 'Your mother's right. Get married. You can have a career alongside too. She managed quite well, didn't she?' He then pales and stops abruptly as the import of his words strikes him.

Mamma managed quite well, too well, perhaps. Did it make it easier to leave her, knowing she was such a good manager?

How's your new wife? She should ask Papa perhaps. It might be impolite if she didn't. But she can only refer to her by her old name, the name they had known her by when she was the friendly neighbour who liked to spend time at their place—the jolly middle-aged lady with brightly-hennaed hair, who made such good samosas, such excellent biryani. So lively, despite the fact that she was a widow with an only son who lived abroad, leaving her all alone with so much money that she was desperate to find someone to share it with her. Funny, she found someone who lived so close by, but then had to move so far away with him. What had won him over—the cooking

(Mamma was equally good), the readiness to exchange jokes, or was it something else?

'How's Mrs Nath?' she finally asks with neutral courtesy, not quite sure why.

Papa, cool customer that he is, replies, 'She's fine ... she likes to call herself Mrs Chopra now.' There's something comically conspiratorial about his smile and an insane giggle escapes her. For a few minutes they both laugh hysterically.

She stops short when she sees Soma passing by. Soma looks disapproving. But later it makes Nitya laugh even more for some reason. Perhaps it's the odd sense of superiority that sweeps over her. Soma doesn't have a father who's run off with another woman and now wears a toupee and natty suede shoes and hands over five thousand rupees to his daughter to have fun with, without turning a hair. Not everyone can dare so much.

'Yes,' Papa repeats. 'She likes to call herself Mrs Chopra now.' He winks as if they share a secret.' She tries to giggle again but she's all laughed out and the sound she produces grates on her ear. 'Maybe she'd like it if you would call her Mummy.'

She turns rigid and even he realizes he's gone too far. She can hear his heavy breathing despite the sounds of conversation all around her. The ordinary normal conversation of ordinary normal people, not of fathers who run off with other women to live as kept men and begin to wear toupees and stylish suede shoes; of grey-haired or bald fathers who count the costs of their children's education and balance it with the salaries they expect to earn later, while planning for their impending retirement alongside.

'I'll send you more money, whenever you need it.' She's about to protest when she sees him expand, throwing her a knowing glance. 'I've taken up a new assignment,' he says. 'They pay very well. I'd like to send Akshay abroad to study—only … I'm afraid your mother wouldn't agree.'

She stares at him for a while before answering. 'Why wouldn't she? She's not the type to stand in our way—you know that!'

'Yes I know that,' he repeats shamefacedly, then lets out a small wisp of a sigh.

She feels an odd prickling underneath the thick sleeves of her cardigan. It's so sharp that she can't move and is compelled to sit frozen to her seat lest it become unbearable. She can barely hear him say, 'All right, Nitu. I'll be seeing you more often. My new job means I have to come regularly to Delhi … Take care.' He stands up, then bends to kiss her on the top of her head. She doesn't wave good-bye or turn to look as he walks away, but moves stiffly towards the stairs that'll take her back to her narrow room and the assignment that seems like a weary burden now instead of a stepping stone to a magical new existence.

Only the shout from a girl behind her, 'Hey, you're dropping your money!' alerts her to the fact that her fist has opened up and the crumpled notes are scudding across the dusty floor like precious wasted hours. She turns to nod her thanks and hurriedly scoops them up.

She's not quite sure how she will spend this money, as she is not sure what it means to her. If she were to consult Soma what would she say? You should have thrown it back in his face, or out of the window, or donated it all to charity?

She knows she wouldn't do any of these things. Because a stubborn belief wedges itself in her—she has a right to it even if she's not sure if she was convinced when he said he had a job. Let Mrs Nath—who wants to be known as Mrs Chopra and even dares to imagine them calling her 'Mummy' now—pay. Pay for her fun and Akshay's education abroad. It's the least she can do.

Acknowledgments

'Cradle Song' first appeared in *The Asian Age* when it won the first prize in their short story competition; 'You Cannot have All the Answers' and 'Visitors' Hour' in *Cicada* magazine, USA; 'The Phalanx' in *Indian Literature* under the title 'After the Floods'; 'Closure' in *The Little Magazine*; 'The Path' in the anthology *Alien Shores* published by Brass Monkey Publishers, Australia; 'The Crossing' in *Manushi*; 'Babies' on the website museindia.com, 'The Back Veranda', 'The Stuff of Dreams', 'If the Earth Should Move', 'The House of Cards', 'Doorways Without Doors' and 'Why Did You Kill Mahatma Gandhi?' in an earlier collection published by Srishti Publishers.